NASTY

FETISH FIGHTS BACK

An Erotic Short Story Collection

EDITED BY ANNA YEATTS & CHRIS PHILLIPS

For information contact:
http://www.thenastymag.com
thenastymag@gmail.com

Book and Cover design by Anna Yeatts
ISBN: 9780692885512

First Edition: May 2017

10 9 8 7 6 5 4 3 2 1

CONTENTS

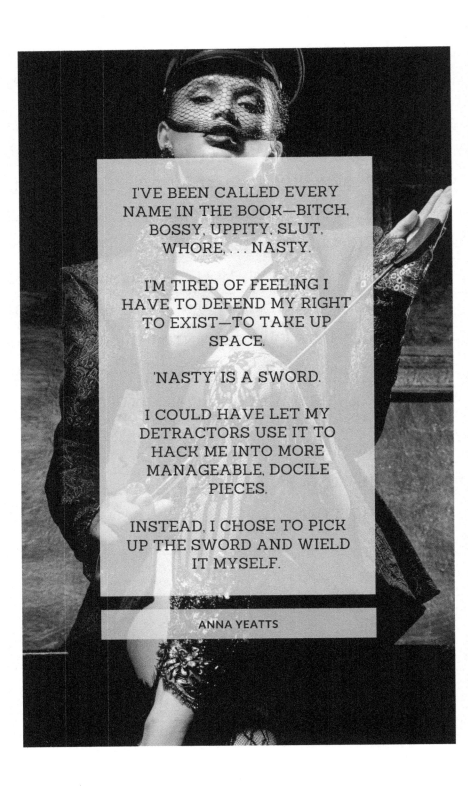

I'VE BEEN CALLED EVERY NAME IN THE BOOK—BITCH, BOSSY, UPPITY, SLUT, WHORE, . . . NASTY.

I'M TIRED OF FEELING I HAVE TO DEFEND MY RIGHT TO EXIST—TO TAKE UP SPACE.

'NASTY' IS A SWORD.

I COULD HAVE LET MY DETRACTORS USE IT TO HACK ME INTO MORE MANAGEABLE, DOCILE PIECES.

INSTEAD, I CHOSE TO PICK UP THE SWORD AND WIELD IT MYSELF.

ANNA YEATTS

FOREWORD

BY ANNA YEATTS

W HY READ THE FOREWORD, RIGHT?
NASTY is a collection of erotic short stories. You have every right to want to dive straight into the sensual gooey-goodness following what I have to say.

Hell, most erotica writers can't even get readers to hang around long enough to read the *plot,* much less a *foreword.* Just get to the sexy bits already!

But NASTY isn't like most collections of erotic short fiction.

And the writers in this book probably are not like any you've read in the past.

So you take a couple of seconds (put the lotion down—no judgment—just hold on) and let me explain.

NASTY has a little of this, and a little of that, and a whole lot of come-as-you-are (no pun intended). I believe that every one of us hanging out on Planet Earth has an equal right to love and be loved. No matter who we choose to love or how we go about it—so long as we're in a consensual, adult relationship—we deserve to be treated with respect and dignity. Sexuality is healthy, natural, and beautiful.

But unlike what I think, mainstream culture has long considered sensuality, when it differs from 'normal,' as a dark and shameful secret.

For some of us that means being gay, transgender, nonbinary, or simply being not-male. Sometimes it gets a bit more complicated. If your sexuality manifests in a less 'normal' way, let's say as a submissive, foot fetishist, or a bondage-enthusiast, the more conservative societal and political factions are quick to heap shame on top of your nastiness.

But at the end of the day, those who shame us for who and how we love are simply out to control the urges they choose not to understand.

Okay, okay, so what does this have to do with not jumping ahead and getting to the sexy stories as fast as possible? Because NASTY: Fetish Fights Back is actually fighting back. It's not just a catchy tagline. For as long as NASTY stays in print, we'll be donating 20% of the profits to Planned Parenthood.

And we hope NASTY is around for a very, very long time.

Planned Parenthood is often smeared as nothing more than an abortion factory selling baby parts on the deep-web black market. If you've spent longer than fifteen minutes online, you've heard the crazy rumors manufactured by alt-right and Moral Majority groups all in the name of "save the babies."

No matter if you're pro-choice or pro-life, the ultimate goal is healthier, happier babies and families. It saddens me when that message is lost amidst propaganda screeds. The whole point of Planned Parenthood is to provide family planning services to low-income women—the very women who, without proper medical care, birth control, and other educational services, could be financially pushed into heartbreaking decisions like should

I end my pregnancy? Planned Parenthood also provides STD screening and treatment, pregnancy tests, prenatal care, PAP smears, mammograms, and even vasectomies. Their contribution to women's health goes far beyond the narrow picture painted by conservative media.

To this end, we asked the best writers in short fiction today to craft stories specifically for NASTY. And did they ever.

The vulnerability, strength, and ultimately, the beauty of the human spirit has rarely been more evident to me than right here in NASTY.

Award-winning horror writer, D.F. Warrick's "The Things I Told the Cops After the Uprising (and a Few Things I Wish I'd Told Them)" is a stunning yet complicated love story. When your body feels foreign and wrong, how do you ask someone else to find you attractive, much less sensual? But this story transported me with so much passion and rawness, at times almost uncomfortably real, I felt I'd been given a glimpse into something so vital, so honest, I didn't want it to be fiction. This was love, acceptance, and I wanted it to be true.

And that is the power of story.

Story lifts us up out of our personal experience and transports us into the eyes, mind, and heart of someone else—someone not like us—so for an instant, we can experience a life that is not like our own.

I hope you find a story in these pages that opens allows you to share the experience of your neighbor.

When Chris Phillips, my co-editor and longtime writing partner, and I decided to follow through and create NASTY, I had no idea what the end product would be. But this collection is more than I ever imagined. It shares our humanity in one of the most beautiful ways possible.

And we've got a little something for everyone.

Die-hard political activists should swing by five-time Bram Stoker Award Winner Lucy A. Snyder's "Devoured," for the sexiest version of eating crow ever. Then skip to the end for Jessica Freely's satirical jab at a certain right-wing politician in "The Straw Man." Every one loves a rugged trucker.

Current John W. Campbell Award Finalist for Best New Writer, Kelly Robson gives us "The Desperate Flesh." Though she swears her story is anything but nasty, it is political, and there are pasty-wearing lesbians you can't help but love. Don't miss Steve Berman's "My Best Dish," a subtle but poignant look at intersectional relationships and, of all things, hot dogs.

And then there was "Dinner with Daniel Coletti" by Nathan Pettigrew. If you grew up in the Bible Belt, I promise you'll get more than a kick out of this one. Hold onto your Bibles and don't say I didn't warn you.

Fancy a bit more science fiction in your steamy? A. Merc Rustad's stunning lyrical prose brings life to "Bodies like Galaxies," an uploading love story among the stars.

"Mechanogenation" by Konstantine Paradias is a man/machine mash-up that gives sex-machine a whole new meaning. Or try "Space Pussy!" by Matthew F. Amati. A retro-fitted, turbocharged vagina never sounded so ... diddle-worthy?

"Masks" by 'Nathan Burgoine explores not only the underground world of bondage and domination but hidden identities, both internal and external. Burgoine deftly reveals both his characters' vulnerabilities and desires in this sleek little gem. A personal favorite of mine.

Tom Cardamone's "Hypoxyphilia" is a surprisingly powerful story I wouldn't expect to find in a traditional erotica collection. When I finished reading this one for the first time, I sat for a moment, collecting both myself and my breath—stunned by its emotional vulnerability, the raw tensions, and Cardamone's authorial craftsmanship.

Another compelling story I immediately loved is "Cold to the Touch" by legendary horror writer, Tim Waggoner. The beautifully woven backstory and emotional complexity plus all the smoking sex in the frigid air is something you have to read to believe.

If you like your erotica hot, hot, hot, turn immediately to "Acts of Contrition" by New York Times Bestseller Selena Kitt, known for her erotic Baumgartner series. Basically, when your stories are turned into adult movies, you know you're batting into the seriously-steamy range. "Acts of Contrition" is a fast-paced spanking that will leave you flushed and ready for more.

Lazuli Jones' "Metal" combines pain and pleasure with a fetish that's increasingly common but not like this. Jones ramps up the sexual chemistry in this deliciously naughty piercing story. When you end up with a new piercing or two, don't say I didn't warn you.

Shirley Jackson Award Winner and horror writer extraordinaire, Gemma Files, best known for her novel Experimental Film, wrote "Somnophilia" for NASTY. So-wrong but so-right, "Somnophilia" evokes the can't look away type of fascination you probably felt the first time you found Joy of Sex stashed in your parents' nightstand. Trust me. Read it.

Rose de Fer's "Breathless" is near and dear to my own dark fetish heart. It's a corset story. (Though I've tried explaining to people that being unlaced from a corset is like smacking a can of instant biscuits on the countertop—that gratifying *FW-PLOP* sound as the cardboard tube explodes outward into dough, let's agree Rose explains it far better). "Breathless" portrays both the sensory and psychological experience of corsetry. And I promise that Rose's delivery is far more desirable and sexy than my biscuit analogy.

Fantasy lovers, we didn't forget about you either! In speculative fiction crossover territory, we have "Galatea" by Cassie

Alexander—a new take on the Pygmalion and Galatea myth but much more detailed (I was going to say tongue-in-cheek because tongues do go lots of places).

Ann Castle brings us "Dendrophilia"—a beautifully written story that makes even parasitic fungus sound like a good idea. I'm not even kidding. When a writer can make fungus hot, you know the skill level is high.

Even cryptids need love and acceptance in "The Stone Beast" by Darien Cox. Granted, I had to ask Chris what cryptids were (fine, judge me, I did), but I finished this story thinking maybe that Big Foot guy was hotter than I gave him credit for being. The Stone Beast leaves Big Foot in the dust with this sultry read.

For more mythological beasts, head over to "Riding Yggdrasil" by Charles Payseur. Once you stop wallowing in the glorious prose, enjoy the magical masturbatory powers we all secretly suspected but never proved.

Or try out some serious laboratory kink with Kaysee Renee Richardson's "Knitted, Knotted, and Besotted." When the fantasy genre collides with hooded bondage, an incredibly talented seamstress, and a film set, the sky is the limit to what might (and does) happen.

And rounding out our cross-genre stories, Lucien Soulban's "Humiliation" takes dominant-submissive roles to another stratosphere all together in this superhero versus supervillain romp with a safe word thrown in for good (or evil?) measure.

Fellow *Flash Fiction Online* staffer and *Triumph for Sakura* author, Jason S. Ridler was conned into writing for NASTY. Check out "Maps for a Worm"—a dark literary story about one man's obsession with women's legs, and especially, their leg veins.

Literary fans will also enjoy "Library Dust" by Robert Brouhard. We all know that person who has the world's cutest sneeze, but what about a sexy sneeze? (Pass the tissues, please.) Enjoy your Dewey Decimal System. We certainly did.

Not enough words for you? "Aural Sex" by bestselling author Jaye Wells takes the love of words to new lengths. Really. Long luscious words literally whet the whistle (chiaroscuro, anyone?) in this sweet yet sexy story.

Or for those of you who like your prose a bit naughtier, try Molly Tanzer's "Prick and Persuasion." Yes, Mister Darcy, I will mend your pen.

And finally, what would a fetish erotica book be without a smoking hot dominatrix? I give you "Please" by Cassandra Khaw. This tiny story packs a wallop. Be prepared. Or not. Sometimes giving in and losing control is the best part.

Whatever you do, I hope you enjoy the stories in NASTY: Fetish Fights Back. Chris and I poured a lot of love (and blood and sweat and ... okay, yes, a tear or two) into this collection, and we're proud to stand behind it.

I've been called Nasty. Slut. Whore. Bossy. Liar. Bitch. If you can think of it, I've been called it. But I'm tired of taking those barbs with my head down. That chapter of my life is over.

I claim NASTY as my right to be who and what I am.

I hope you do too.

All my best,
Anna Yeatts
Publisher and Co-Editor of *NASTY: Fetish Fights Back*

Devoured

by Lucy A. Snyder

$\mathcal{P}$ANIC AND SHAME NIPPED AT VELOURIA'S HEART as she hurried down the cobblestone alley. The mob's mocking chants echoed only distantly, but she could smell torches and tar. The terrified look on Mother Cotton's face as the Purity Watch tore her robes from her body would surely haunt Velouria the rest of her life. The sorceress' apprentice fled before they poured boiling pitch and feathers upon the poor witch.

It's not my fault, she tried to convince herself. But in her heart, she knew it was. And her mistress would be furious if she found out.

Velouria tried scrubbing the tell-tale orange balloteer's stamp off the back of her left hand. The threadbare hem of her robe didn't even smear the ink. Perhaps she could find some whiskey or a bit of turpentine to remove it before anyone saw–

She was nearly blinded by a cobalt flash in the night, and suddenly Lady Euphrates was standing before her, inky eyes fierce and unforgiving. Velouria's breath caught in her throat. Her

8

mistress was glorious in her shimmering purple robes. She was a handsome woman, certainly, but the sudden quickening Velouria felt in her chest and loins wasn't due to any mundane beauty. Lady Euphrates radiated sheer power, a dark sunshine that the apprentice yearned to bask in. Velouria so thoroughly adored the simple act of being in her lady's presence that sometimes she thought she might faint. To think of ever touching her mistress, or being touched by her ... it was too much. She couldn't voice her desire to anyone, not even her fellow apprentice Isla. Not even after they'd giggled over girls they fancied and shared lingering kisses in alcoves of the training library.

Velouria reflexively covered the balloteer's mark with her right hand and curtsied low, wishing she had some way to hide her blushing. "Mistress."

"Show me your hand."

"Mistress, I–"

"Now."

Face hot with mortification, Velouria slowly raised her trembling hand so that her mistress could see that she had voted for their new governor Urtico. Lady Euphrates' face hardened into disappointed anger. "How could you betray us like that? How could you be so infernally *stupid?*"

"I didn't think–"

"Obviously!" Her mistress threw up her hands in disgust.

"He promised lower taxes. I thought the Purity Watch was just a bluster to get the troglodyte vote," Velouria protested weakly. "This city's renowned for its witches and wizards–I couldn't imagine he was serious about casting us out."

Lady Euphrates stepped closer and dropped her voice to a wintery whisper. "When a politician tells you he plans to do something terrible? *Believe him.*"

Velouria's shame was an itching demon she was desperate to exorcise. "There are a hundred thousand people in the city," she pleaded. "Surely, I alone, did not put Urtico in power!"

"No clod in a mudslide feels responsible for the homes it crushes," Lady Euphrates' voice was bitterly cold.

"I'm ... I'm sorry." Velouria bowed her head.

"Sorry isn't good enough. Mother Cotton's just been stripped of her dignity and citizenship and burned half to death. I've spent nearly 500 pounds to make sure that she gets a proper healing and a carriage to transport her safely to Breven Town. Have you the 500 pounds to repay me? Have you even 50?"

Tears arose in Velouria's eyes. "You know I don't, Mistress."

Lady Euphrates knelt and spoke in Velouria's ear, agonizingly close. The apprentice's heartbeat fluttered like a hummingbird's. "Mother Cotton did *nothing* to deserve what they did to her. What you ran away from. You couldn't even watch what your vote bought us all! What do you think *you* deserve?"

"I deserve to be p-punished," Velouria wept.

"Yes. You do." Lady Euphrates stood, glowering majestically over her. "Arrive at the Oaken Pony Tavern at sundown. Tell them your party is in the basement. Dress well, but do not expect your clothes to survive the night. And do not be late."

✺ ʔ ✺

Velouria smoothed the bodice of her maroon gown nervously as the serving girl led her down the creaking stairs to the tavern's basement. What was Lady Euphrates going to do to her? No apprentice had ever displeased her like this before. Velouria had briefly considered running away, but her mistress' hunting magic was legendary. She could no more escape her wrath than a rabbit on a slippery glacier could outrun an eagle.

"Your party awaits, milady."

10

The serving girl pushed open the heavy door and held it wide.

Heart skittering, Velouria stepped through. She was in a curving corridor. Torchlight flickered on bare plaster walls. Her stomach dropped when the sturdy door thudded shut behind her ... and she had to fight off a spike of outright panic at the clack of the lock.

There was nothing to do but to meet her fate. She slowly walked down the tenebrous hallway, tension winding more tightly inside her with every step. Not just tension, but a buzzing anticipation spreading through her chest and belly down to her loins. Her mistress was going to punish her. It would be painful, no doubt, and probably humiliating ... but Lady Euphrates might put her hands upon her. She'd dreamed of that on so many nights. Being slapped in righteous anger, being thrown to the ground, that was still a touch, wasn't it? That sort of raw brutality wasn't in the Lady's nature, as far as Velouria knew. But she was certain she could endure any pain if it meant feeling her mistress' hand upon her.

The corridor opened into a banquet hall. A single enchanted torch hovered above the near end of a tall oak table. Below the light was a single plate piled high with roasted fowl. There were no chairs at the table. The torch was the only light, and its illumination didn't carry very far into the rest of the room.

"Your dinner awaits." Lady Euphrates' voice seemed to be everywhere. "You're not allowed out of here until you finish."

Velouria cautiously approached plate upon the table. Three game birds sat on a bed of glossy black leaves. The birds were about the size of Cornish hens, but longer and leaner than usual and glazed in an orange-colored sauce that uncomfortably reminded her of her balloteer's mark. It was quite a bit of fowl to consume in one sitting, but she could manage. There wasn't any cutlery-she'd have to dine with her fingers.

Velouria blinked. The leaves were feathers. Crow feathers. She'd been served roasted crow.

"Isla, begin." Lady Euphrates said.

Velouria turned as her fellow apprentice stepped from the shadows. She wasn't wearing a single stitch, and Velouria felt jelly-kneed at the sight of her high, dark-nippled breasts and the curling thatch of her privates. It took her a moment to notice the gleaming shears the apprentice gripped in her left hand.

"W-what are you doing?" Velouria asked.

"Silence," said Lady Euphrates.

Isla strode up and grabbed the cuff of Velouria's sleeve. "Say the word 'scarlet' and I'll stop," Isla murmured softly between barely parted lips. "But you do have to finish your birdies."

Velouria stood shocked as Isla slit the entire length of her sleeve with one expert swoop of the shears.

"Eat your crow," her mistress ordered from the shadows.

Velouria snatched up the first lean bird and twisted off a glazed leg, expecting it to be tough and rancid. But to her delight, she discovered that the bird was tender and well-cooked. It smelled delicious. But it was hard to hold onto the slippery fowl as Isla tugged and snipped away at her clothing, exposing her bit by bit to the chilly room.

"You're a wicked, foolish, selfish apprentice, and you should feel ashamed!" Isla dramatically ripped the skirt from Velouria's hips, and Velouria gasped as the cold air touched her legs.

And she did feel ashamed–here she was, nearly stripped bare in front of her mistress. Her hot blush made her a watchtower beacon of embarrassment.

"Wicked!" Isla delivered a stinging barehanded slap to her buttocks. The blow sent a tingling shock straight into her nethers and she gasped and nearly dropped her bird. For one brief second, she thought of speaking scarlet, but decided that she would not add cowardly to her list of flaws.

"Eat!" Lady Euphrates thundered.

Velouria finally took a hasty bite of the crow's tender leg. At first, she tasted savory herbs and rich oils ... and then the spice. Oh, sweet Goddess, the peppery sauce blazed like smoking lava. She gasped for air around the meat, searching the table in vain for a glass of water to cool her tortured tongue, but there was none. The heat spread from her mouth through her entire body, and in two quick heartbeats sweat beaded from every pore.

"Wicked," Isla whispered as she cut away her underthings.

Velouria trembled and tried to focus on nothing except her fiery meal as Isla ran her fingers softly over her slick, goose-bumped skin. The spice was making her light-headed, euphoric. Her fingers were tingling and her lips swollen. If she finished she could leave. They had said so. But part of her didn't want to leave. Isla's touch was delicious, and more than she had let herself imagine. The embarrassment of being naked before her mistress was more torture than the peppery fowl, but it was a kind of ecstasy, too.

Isla ducked beneath the table. What did she mean to do? The girl took hold of the backs of her thighs, pulled her body tight to the edge of the table, and kissed her vulva. Velouria gave an astonished cry and her vision went scarlet, scarlet as Isla's tongue worked its way into her most secret places, scarlet, it was a good word, but she would not say it, she would eat her blazing crow and suck the bones because she could not reach Isla's nipples to suck upon them, scarlet, her world had gone scarlet with the fire inside.

Her knees giving way, she teetered backward, but she felt her mistress' strong hands upon her naked shoulders, and oh, it was too much, and she wailed as the orgasm took her so strongly that for a moment she blacked out.

When Velouria's senses returned, she found herself lying upon a blanket on the floor. Isla and Lady Euphrates hovered over her, wearing expressions of concern. She couldn't see what remained upon the table.

"Did I finish my crow?" Her tongue and lips were so swollen from the spice it was painful to speak.

Lady Euphrates nodded. "You did. You ate every last morsel. You can go. But you should lie still a bit longer. For safety."

"If this was my punishment for being very bad," Velouria asked, "what shall happen if I am very good?"

Isla and her mistress smiled and exchanged glances.

"If you are ever very good," her mistress replied, "then I'm sure you shall find out."

Dendrophilia

BY ANN CASTLE

GRETA'S DREAMS ARE FULL OF TREES AND passionate kisses with men sprouting branches and leaves. Fungal threads fill her mouth and dissolve like cotton candy, and she wakes gasping and wet with need.

Her recent trysts have left her unsatisfied and lonely. She's tired of men afraid of the mouth-to-mouth contact that transmits the fungus, tired of the way they jerk away from her when she tries to kiss them, longing for connection. She needs a man who's already infected, but they're supposed to be quarantined.

If her life didn't feel so empty, if she didn't want to join the forest, she'd have given up.

Instead, Greta hunted parts of the Internet she never knew existed--she's not the only person who's seeking the fungus-- and eventually set up a date. Now she stands on the cafe's patio, watching hungry maple branches sway over the tables.

Her recently infected date is easy to spot. His photo was accurate, but it's his expression that identifies him: appetite and emptiness his expensive suit can't hide. The fungus peers from his eyes, searching for a way to spread.

It sees her, and the man's eyes widen. His lips part. Greta's breaths come faster even as her steps slow. It's not too late to leave. Not too late to live.

Her vision fills with green branches stretching toward the sun. Desire—for sex, for *belonging*—makes her hands tremble and her knees weaken.

She wants to be part of something greater than herself. She joins him at his small table.

The man has no obvious signs of infection, no white threads running across his skin or poking from his mouth, but his eyes keep drifting to her lips. They don't make small talk for long. He asks, "Are you sure?"

"Yes," she murmurs. She runs her tongue across the roof of her mouth, the back of her lips, imagining fungal tendrils caressing her. Soon. Beneath the table, her legs spread.

"You know what will happen." It's not a question. He's leaning forward, the fungus inside him trying to reach her across the table. "Have you seen the videos?"

God, she's *memorized* every bootleg video of the forest orgies. The fungus drives its victims to the trees, where they couple until they die. A white web of fungal tendrils spreads over the corpses, siphoning nutrients through the soil to the roots of the oaks and maples that tower over the mass graves.

Greta stares at the hungry branches overhead and licks her lips. Her hand drifts down between her legs. "We'll become part of a huge ecosystem. They've found human DNA in trees miles from any orgy sites. It's beautiful."

"It's horrifying," the man whispers.

It's both, and Greta needs to be part of it.

The moment their hotel room's door closes, the man presses Greta against it and kisses her. It's the most amazing kiss she's ever experienced. Knowing the fungus is what's making her feel good makes it even better. The man's tongue presses against hers, and threads tickle the inside of her mouth as the fungus caresses her from inside, piercing her skin. She holds him tight, every nerve screaming for release.

After the rush of that kiss, it's hard to believe anything could be better. He slides down her body, pulling her trousers off on the way, and takes her in his mouth. The fungus touches her, and Greta cries out with pleasure. Her vision darkens—as if leaves cover her eyes—and she gasps for air, the fungus wriggling in her mouth and throat. Something, tongue or tendril, slips inside her, and she arches her back, needing more, giving all of herself to the forest.

She whimpers when he pulls away, though the fungus still caresses her, burrowing deeper. He stands, and she wraps a leg around his waist as he pushes himself into her. The fungus inside her vibrates in counterpoint to his thrusts. Her pleasure builds with every stroke, spreading to every inch of her body.

With a grunt, he comes. Tendrils move between them, filling her, and Greta imagines the fungus burrowing through her. She screams as her own orgasm hits, screams until her lungs are empty, wishes she didn't need to stop to breathe. They collapse together, panting.

She feels her desire rising again almost as soon as he pulls out, but it's not him she wants, or her doing the wanting. It's the fungus urging her to spread it to others.

Greta, like her date, could fight it for a time. She won't become mindlessly desperate for days. But she doesn't want to go through the motions of normal life, doesn't want to die in quarantine.

Doesn't have to feel alone anymore.

⤛ ⸙ ⤜

She packs her car and heads for the woods. Greta hears the infected before she sees them, every moan speeding her steps across the uneven forest floor. She stumbles over rotting bodies covered in thick white webs that hide the decay. Bright sunlight flickers over the fungus as wind ruffles the leaves overhead. She sheds her clothes as she walks. The grunts and cries grow louder, the bodies more exposed, until finally, she reaches people still writhing in desperate ecstasy.

A hand wraps around her bare ankle. She stops, surrounded by people in various stages of sex and decay, and looks up. Around her oaks and maples rise to the sky, a vast web of interconnected trees.

Greta tries to take another step, but her foot sticks, held to the forest floor by a mass of white tendrils. It's already beginning.

At the thought, a tremor of desire runs through her, sending her to her knees. She kisses the nearest person, winding her hands in a woman's black hair, the fungus moving between their mouths. Greta leans into the kiss, pressing the moaning woman back. The woman bucks, and Greta realizes she's riding a man, his body already covered in white. She slides her hand down the woman's body and caresses her, then the man, her hand moving back and forth between them.

She's not in control of herself anymore. Someone presses into her from behind, and she spreads her legs wider. Fungus tangles her fingers where she's touching the other two, and she couldn't pull her hand away even if she wanted to.

Pinpricks tickle her shins. She looks down and back, sees tendrils burrowing into her bare legs, holding her to the ground. It feels glorious.

Greta looks up at the trees. Soon she'll be part of them, part of this beautiful ancient organism. She shivers in pleasure. As the fungus takes its final hold on her, her thoughts fade away, and Greta's body fucks mindlessly, waiting to belong to the forest.

HYPOXYPHILIA

BY TOM CARDAMONE

Y THROAT IS LIKE A FIST.

Maybe it's more the wrist, that root of power and dexterity that grows into the hand.

The hand on my throat. Something of an ouroboros? Looping, headless, swallowing itself in a blind clasp? I imagine a wristwatch on a veiny arm impossibly bent in on itself, an eyeless lock of two hands growing out of one another.

I must be running out of oxygen, so I tap out. He's heavy atop me, crushing my penis into a flaccid conduit of building tension and old laments. Sweaty hand on the taut thigh of my unnamed partner, a wispy tap, what he must think is a caress, a bit of urging onward, to keep choking me. But that's not what I want. (It's completely and utterly what I want, to be pushed to the edge of need, and now I need air. I must breathe. I must surface, having so luxuriated at the silty bottom of consciousness.) But he doesn't heed my call, and so I scratch, thinking the bite of my nails will elicit attention and that elicits only anger and a tighter squeeze, and really, I'm all out of options, aren't I? I mean, I have no voice in this situation, do I? One of the few blessed moments where I am unable to express myself, bark an order, exude a sigh, all of that is taken by the hand on my throat.

Choking, I wish I could swallow and find it ironic that this man's incidental drool has whetted my lips.

I quit slapping his thighs and grip the mattress as his cock knocks about in my ass. His back arches and his legs go straight, and I can tell he's cumming, and once again I don't feel any internal piercing, what my friend Jeff calls "hot arrows"—he loves it when men cum inside him, exalts in it, exclaims he can feel the threads lance his hollows, and yet I feel nothing but relief as the weight crashing down on my abdomen and torso heralds the liberation of the hand from my throat—that which unties all that binds my tense body and fractured mind and an exquisite orgasm is released: a flock of skittish birds that scatter, shattering my shoulders to fly out of my upturned chin as I shoot but not this time.

This time my unnamed guest, via Adam4Adam, kicking off his shoes as I shut the door, mouth open, looking past me, already fixated on the promised mount and rut, of my texted assurance that my body was his to abuse.

Now he forgets to let go and so I go black around the eyes again, the narrowing of vision, the wings of said birds reaching toward each other instead of the sky and with frayed feathers the light shrinks and I feel bad that I didn't pay the rent yet, that there is a week's worth of unopened mail on the dining room table, that I forgot to text Jeff a picture of my trick and the promise to call while the cum is cooling in my cavity, a glass of red wine in hand as I relive every detail over the phone. (Jeff always returns the favor. Our adventures the same but different. He hunts in parks and midnight parking garages, so I get text messages of census and locale that, if read aloud, sound as if delivered by the disembodied narrator of a weird nature show: "Park mostly empty. Winter means no leaves, so no cover. Four guys fighting over one top. I'm horny but willing to wait. It is cold but more guys will appear after bars close." Though I never get pictures, once he accidentally called me on his cell phone while in the middle of a fuck and I could hear their noises, the rummaging around in one another's bodies like bears rooting through tipped over trash cans.)

I gasp.

Lost in the heady swirl of his own spent ecstasy, this man doesn't get it, that his hand on my throat will accidentally erase my soul. Then he shifts and instinctively I suck in air and my erection swells and with a cough I excrete jagged bursts of semen and he looks at me quizzically, as if I were somehow overacting.

He rises in one bound and struggles to pull his pants on. Though I drew the shades, some late afternoon sun slips in and glints off his silver wristwatch. Stretching and shaking on the bed, sheets long ago pushed down by desperate legs, two drowning men trying to gain traction in the sea of each other, I clench my hands. My palms open like a flower, the flower of a fist that holds a secret only someone else can release, tease out of me, a truth that needs another to be heard.

My fist is like a throat.

Bodies Like Galaxies

by A. Merc Rustad

SENSATION UNWINDS LIKE SILK, SPOOLED OUT FROM the body and pulled taut across infinity. You have skin bright as the Milky Way, able to experience every breath of the stars, every caress of planets; hollow space licks eon—scented dust from your lips; you slide your fingers through the void, teasing it towards climax. Your lover, another galaxy, wraps around you, inside you, fucking you as only a galaxy can: huge and hot and endless.dy, and she wakes gasping and wet with need.

>m ? m<

"You ever loaded up?" Kim asked, eyeing me over their mug of hot ginger and honey tea.

"Like 'uploaded'?" I said.

"Yeah." Kim teased the tip of their tongue between their lips and hooded their eyelids.

I squirmed in my chair. "Considering the machinery and

22

procedure is grounded in physical space, I don't know that it's any less real than—"

Kim laughed and threw a crumpled napkin at my head. "Dork. Seriously, Mads. Have you tried it?"

"Nah. Don't think it's my, um, thing."

"Well." They reached back into their purse and teased out a slim white envelope. They leveled it in front of their face so all I could see were their eyes, accented by violet eyeliner. "Guess what I got us for the weekend?"

Kim handed me the envelope. I opened it, and a pair of tickets to UPLOAD FANTASY slid out.

Kim smirked. "I'm a loaded virgin, too."

I took a breath. Kim's sense of adventure was one of the ten thousand things I loved about them, and one way or another they always ended up roping me into their experiments.

Sometimes we used actual rope.

><~ 9 ~><

Imagine the gravity wells of black holes: they slow time and pull your awareness out like insatiable tongues licking deeper, finding the wettest crevices, lapping you up and swallowing you—so slow, so deep. Mouths kissing your infinite skin. Inhaling your breath and body. The pressure from collapsing matter devouring you in swirls of light.

><~ 9 ~><

I didn't have a quantifiably good relationship with my family. I'd been dating Kim six months and had grown tired of having to correct not-so-well-meaning relatives on our pronouns. Finally, at Christmas, I made a card and sent one to everyone.

It was three panels on 6x9 glossy stock. It started with a picture of me, and the caption in bold red letters: MAD(I)S(ON) IS A MAN. DON'T

BE THAT ASSHOLE ABOUT IT. Then a picture of Kim: KIM IS GENDERQUEER, AND THEIR PRONOUNS ARE THEY/THEM/THEIR. IT'S NOT THAT HARD TO REMEMBER.

The third panel was a hand-drawn illustration of an erect penis and a strap-on making kissy faces at each other. Caption:

Just because Kim has a cock and Mads has a cunt doesn't make them cishet. Stop being dicks about their genders and genitals and fuck off. Happy holidays!

Kim and I both put on hot pink lipstick, kissed each card so the lip-prints overlapped, and mailed them off. Kim snapped a pic of the card and updated all their social media profiles.

No one in the family talked to us after that, which suited me fine.

All that's to say ... even though I hadn't talked to my parents in over a year, I still couldn't shake the sense of their disapproval at the idea of 'loading. What if something went wrong? It was still fairly underground, yet most of my friends raved about it. UPLOAD FANTASY was the biggest center, located behind a classy nightclub downtown. I'd avoided the subject when it came up at parties or dinner with friends.

There'd been no reported side effects or negative health issues, but given that uploading wasn't as widespread or cishet-approved, I wouldn't be surprised if people kept issues to themselves. My unease could be attributed to first-time jitters.

I didn't want to let Kim down when they'd gone through the trouble of getting on the wait list for tickets. They'd be there. I wouldn't be alone in this.

Kim dressed in an adorable leather mini-skirt, a tux jacket with a lacy open-fronted shirt underneath, and black boots up to their thighs. I put on low-cut jeans, a leather tank top with silver chain trim, and my favorite white fedora. We made a fucking badass couple as we took the bus downtown and headed up 5th Ave towards UPLOAD FANTASY.

꙳ ⸮ ꙳

When you first become a galaxy, you are endless. You stretch across imagination and time, beholding the creation of suns and heavens. You are filled with stars and possibility. You taste the passion of supernovas: relish the heat that blooms across your skin, thrusting deep inside and alighting your nerves. Neurons flow like solar winds, looping into circles until you feel yourself in everything. Until you are everything.

Your lover's here: another galaxy—you slide into each other, exchanging a kiss of stars. Your lover twines their fingers into your senses, strokes your mind with eternal affection, and in turn, you wind your tongue about theirs. You taste the span of eons as life evolves. Life is raw, hot, strong—a need you must satiate.

꙳ ⸮ ꙳

I knew the woman who was our chaperone for the upload. We'd been high school sweethearts, but she preferred girls to guys, so we just stayed friends. "Mads!" Elisa said with a grin, giving me a hug.

"God, I've not seen you in months, bro! How's life?"

"Good," I told her. "Kim got us tickets. First time for us."

"Awesome," Elisa said. "Trust me, you'll love it."

"Counting on that," Kim said with a wicked smile.

Elisa led us back to a small room that looked rather like a cheap motel—two narrow beds, digitized paintings along the walls, no windows. But it had cozy, soothing blue wallpaper, and the beds were memory-foam covered in the softest microfiber sheets I'd ever felt.

We took off our boots, and Elisa gave us the rundown as she

hooked us to the upload gear: flexible helmets rather like shower caps, except veined with microchips and wiring.

"When you're ready, I'll activate the load-caps. The caps map your brainwaves and project a copy of yourself into the server."

Kim and I each lay back on a bed. We clasped hands. I hoped they didn't feel me sweating.

"It's not truly 'uploading' in a sense that we don't take you out of your body," Elisa said as one of the wall paintings became a monitor to track vital signs. "You're just experiencing a projection of your own self in a virtual setting. When you come down, that copy is sent back to you—all the experiences intact but familiarized with your own neural patterns so you won't have disassociation. And no, we keep no copies. You're just borrowing the tech to experience a high. Except it's not addicting. Weird thing I noticed was that I don't crave it more than once every few weeks. There's this satisfaction that just ... *lasts.*" She stepped back. "You folks ready?"

"Yep!" Kim said.

I took a breath. Kim was right beside me. They kept hold of my hand. "Okay."

"This room is private, no recording of any sort, and I'm the only tech you'll see. When you come down, those beds can merge, and I'll step out. You're booked for two hours, so take your time. We find that most people get *really* good orgasms after the loading." She winked. "There's condoms, lube, and other accessories in the locker beside the beds. Compliments of the house."

"Let's do this," I said.

⌇ 9 ⌇

When you are done being the Milky Way, Andromeda, Centaurus A, and so many others, you spiral back, compressing yourself into the exquisite masterpiece of a human body: a galaxy contained in skin. Atoms compile. Mass transforms itself, a billion miracles whirling and reshaping until familiar patterns emerge: hands, eyes, ribs, mouths, bodies.

You return to yourself, memory etched in wonder, breathless, and you carry the knowledge that you are celestial in whatever form you take.

I gasped. My whole being, every micron of skin, throbbed with need. It was delicious: the faintest current of air, the mint of Kim's breath—spicy on my cheek—the plush weight of flesh wrapped about bones. I ran my hands over my arms and throat, shivering with ecstasy. Each nerve was alive, bright, and whole. I was hungry; I needed another set of hands on my body. Kim sat up, and our beds merged into one queen-sized expanse. We got rid of clothes, and I pulled Kim on top of me—their cock was inside me, and I wrapped my arms and legs around them. I teased my fingers into their ass, pushing them harder against me. Their mouth was velvet and mine was fire.

I twined my tongue against theirs. I could still taste the stars.

I knew exactly how I was going to illustrate our next Christmas card.

We were galaxies in human form, and we fucked like only galaxies can.

AURAL SEX

BY JAYE WELLS

*W*ORDS EXCITED HER.

Pretty words. Scandalous words. Words that tasted delicious on the tongue.

She loved them shouted, groaned, or even whispered.

Her first orgasm happened sophomore year of college in an art history survey class taught by the handsome Dr. Phillips. During a lecture on Caravaggio, he lingered over the word *chiaroscuro.*

She came instantly.

Luckily, it was an 8 a.m. class, and the room was dark. She covered her moan with a coughing fit and escaped to the restroom. In the smudged mirror over the sink, she caressed her flushed cheeks and whispered the word—*chiascuro*—over and over, like a prayer.

The second time was weeks later when they reached the Impressionism unit, and Dr. Phillips had taken great joy in saying the word *pointillism* in the French manner.

Pwan-tah-lism.

After class, he called her to his office, where he gave her the third orgasm of her life by whispering various art movements against her clitoris. She didn't make it past Fauvism.

Later, she started skulking around other school departments for her titillation, her fix.

The English Lit students gathered on the third floor of the school library to debate the merits of various authors and poets. Desperate to prove themselves, they trotted out their biggest words in a game of syllabic one-upmanship.

"Don Quixote was, like, a peripatetic Diogenes, seeking the truth."

She never sat close enough for them to witness her eager eavesdropping. They never saw her cheeks flush or her hand's slow descent into the valley of her sex. She didn't want to watch them, anyway. She just wanted to listen to the swirl and swagger of consonants and vowels.

When someone inevitably trotted out Shakespeare, her fingers danced against her fevered skin in the iambic pentameter of Elizabethan sonnets.

But after she'd heard the same arguments, the same sonnets, the same five-dollar words spouted by two-dollar intellects, she moved on to other departments, other languages, other honeyed voices. After college, she tried dating a book editor, but that, too, ended in disappointment. He chanted words like *dénouement* into her sensitive ears over and over while digging into her panties with all the grace of a bear clawing for honey in a dead hive. He never understood.

It wasn't that words were *foreplay*. Words were *sex itself*.

Once, desperate, she listened to Neruda's poems using the text-to-speech function on her laptop. Alas, the experience left her feeling hollow and ashamed. Such gorgeous words required tender delivery from a lover's tongue.

The first great irony of her life was accepting a job at the local library. But occasionally, an author would come through and do a reading. Since she worked the events, they were exquisite torture as she struggled to hide her stimulation.

She'd always be alone. Easier that way. Simpler. With the internet, she could easily download videos of her favorite writers and philosophers orating their gorgeous word-porn. Simple. Easy.

Boring.

It was a dreary autumn morning when she found true love hidden inside a journal left behind on her desk-a library patron probably left it by accident. Inside, someone had written a collection of poems and lists in a seductive, if disciplined, hand. She opened to a center page. The heading read simply, "Beautiful Words."

Demesne
Halcyon
Labyrinthine
Mellifluous
Panoply
Sumptuous
Serendipity
Fecund

She clenched her teeth against a groan.

In the back of the journal, she found a small note listing the name "A. Caverly" and an email address.

Writing the email took her three hours. She had to get the wording just right. When she was finally ready to send it, her finger trembled on the mouse.

She didn't sleep that night. She lay on top of her sheets, embracing the silence as a form of reconciliation.

When she arrived the next day, a brief response waited in her inbox.

You have saved my life. Please meet me tonight at Café Harmony at 7 p.m.

It was the longest day of her life. She resisted the urge to imagine the timbre of A. Caverly's voice. She spent her lunch hour reading each poem in the journal. Memorizing them. Resisting the urge to sneak away to the bathroom to relieve her tension.

Café Harmony squatted between an art gallery and a bookstore. The slim space held a tiny stage, a couple of ratty couches, and a coffee bar with an antique espresso maker. When she arrived, only two people were in the café—a woman lounging on a sapphire velvet settee and a man with a thick beard worked behind the coffee bar. She recognized neither of them from the library.

She went straight to the bar and asked for a *café con leche* like her Puerto Rican grandmother had made for her as a girl.

The man with the beard nodded but said nothing. Belatedly, she noticed the name tag on his breast that identified him as Duncan.

He's not my A. Caverly.

A butterfly touch on her shoulder distracted her from her disappointment. She turned. The woman from the couch stood behind her.

The woman had long onyx hair and cerulean eyes that sparkled from behind cat-eye glasses. Her dress left her soft arms bare and revealed a mosaic of words tattooed into her pale flesh.

In her hand, she held a notepad, which she offered with a smile.

My name is Alexis Caverly. I am deaf, but I can read lips.

She looked up. "You can?" she said aloud.

Alexis nodded, her smile wider now. She tapped a black-tipped fingernail against the pad.

She kept reading. *Thank you for bringing my journal. It's my most prized possession.*

Her disappointment was as cumbersome as the Oxford English Dictionary. Alexis loved words, but she could not speak them.

Alexis touched her hand and gave her a knowing frown.

"I'm sorry, I just—I didn't know."

Alexis pointed to the pad again. At the bottom of the page, there were more words. They said, *I'm sorry if this is forward of me, but I have visited the library many times and admired you.*

A blush heated her from chest to forehead, but she kept reading, devouring the simple words.

The poems in the journal are about you.

She glanced up—shocked. How had she missed seeing this woman? Alexis met her searching gaze boldly, unashamed by her desire.

"I never saw you," she said.

Alexis nodded. "I know," she mouthed. She nodded again to the book. *I left the journal for you. It is a love letter.*

Her legs shaking, she sat on the couch, ignoring Duncan's call when her coffee was ready. Alexis paid for it and set it in front of her on the table.

She thanked her and swallowed a bracing sip.

Alexis sat beside her and watched her through those glasses. Her eyes were kind and knowing as if the lenses allowed her to see more than she should.

"I'm sorry," she said. "Your poems are beautiful." So are you. As she thought these words, she recognized them as true. She found Alexis irresistible from her adorable, funky appearance to the way she mastered words like a loving dominatrix.

Besides, some of her best sexual experiences had been women, who were more focused on exploration than conquering. She never liked traditional labels, so she simply considered herself a "lexi-sexual"—turned on by words.

Alexis touched her knee. The contact created a tiny spark. "What's wrong?" she mouthed.

She couldn't say the words aloud. She took Alexis's pad and wrote.

You are beautiful, but I am broken.

Tears fell.

We all are, Alexis wrote back. Where is your wound?

She touched her ear. Then she wrote: *The only medicine I've found is words.*

Alexis smiled sadly and touched her heart. Then she wrote, Words are my medicine too.

Alexis took her hand and led her out of the café and up narrow stairs to a small apartment. She didn't object when the clothes came off, or when she was pushed onto the bed.

Alexis couldn't say the words, but she could spell them across her skin using gentle fingertips or her seeking, soft tongue. Over the rise of her hip, she spelled *L-O-N-G-I-N-G.* Each letter, a promise, heating her skin and making her ache for the next.

Along her spine, she spelled *P-A-S-S-I-O-N.*

The inner thigh became a canvas for *A-L-A-B-A-S-T-E-R.*

By the time Alexis reached her sex, she writhed with excitement.

Alexis used her tongue to write a cursive *L.*

She squeezed her eyes closed.

An exquisite letter *O.*

The seeds of lightning took root in her core.

A swirly, elaborate *V.*

Tendrils of energy wrapped around her spine, rising, rising.

She tattooed the final letter on her sensitive skin with a flourish—an elaborate, elegant *E.*

The orgasm lifted her hips from the bed. Her soul leaped from her skin to dance on the ceiling with shifting shadows and fragmented words. As she sunk back into herself, she felt both rooted and free for the first time in her life.

She tasted herself on Alexis's lips and the salt of tears she hadn't noticed.

She told Alexis all of her secrets with that salty kiss. After a lifetime of yearning to hear, she realized what she'd needed all along was to allow herself to *feel*.

BREATHLESS

BY ROSE DE FER

IFTEEN INCHES. MY FANTASY AND MY GOAL. And I'm close—so close. One more inch and I'll be there.

Just the thought of it makes me lightheaded. Unless that's the already-constricting fifteen inches the corset has compressed my waist into.

Wait, did you think I was talking about something else? Ah. Clearly you don't know me very well.

Yes, what does it for me is the crush of steel bones against my ribs, the slow, firm compression of my body, the focused whittling of my waist. The exquisite confinement and the sense of utter helplessness.

As my master pulls the laces tighter, I become slightly dizzy. I always imagine I might swoon like some delicate Victorian lady. But I never do. I'm much hardier than I look.

My soft curves vanish beneath the silken cage of the scarlet corset, and I grip the bedpost as he draws the laces in more, cinching me smaller and smaller, tighter and tighter. I gasp at the pulse of excitement between my legs, the dampening of my sex. I close my eyes, losing myself in the sensation of his absolute control over me.

Inch by inch, he trained me, gradually getting me used to the rigors of tight-lacing. I prepared for the challenge, the glamour, the suffering for a very particular fashion. But I never expected the deep submission it would bring out in me. The almost unbearable arousal.

Gradually, the panels close at the back. When they meet, the corset as tight as it will go, he will measure my waist. Then he will fuck me.

My body jerks, tugged by his firm, strong fingers as he pulls the laces through the eyelets. My submission deepens with each tightening. It's not just my waist shrinking, but my whole body—as though he laces me down to the size of a tiny pet he can hold in his hand. I love being so completely at his mercy.

He instructs me to take a deep breath, and I obey as best I can. My lungs can no longer fully inflate. The sensation used to frighten me, but with fear comes exhilaration. It's a crucial part of the ritual. After I have drawn in as much air as I can, I release it all, making my torso as small as possible. As I exhale, he pulls the laces again, and I gasp as the corset constricts even tighter. It is how you tighten the girth on a horse's saddle: you wait for the horse to breathe out then pull the straps taut. The idea of being ridden makes me blush, and I sway a little and have to clutch the bedpost again.

He laughs behind me, and his hands slip down over my bottom, stroking the soft flesh there. The lacy edge of the corset frames me nicely for him. Will he fuck me there too? I press my thighs together at the thought.

At last he is done. He takes my hand and leads me before the full-length mirror so we can admire the sight together. My breasts, heaving with each shallow breath I take, swell above the top of the corset. The exaggerated hourglass silhouette emphasizes my breasts and bottom while still drawing the eye to my tiny wasplike waist. I'm beautiful. Kinky.

Such exquisite perversion.

My master passes the tape around my waist and reads the measurement. "Sixteen inches." He smiles. "Good girl."

My sex pulses hungrily, responding to the pride in his voice. When he encircles my waist, his fingers meet with room to spare. He cups my breasts over the silk of the bodice. I barely feel his touch through the material, but the barrier only intensifies my arousal. My nipples are painfully hard beneath it. It's a strange sort of bondage, wholly restrictive and confining, yet wildly liberating. I'm lost somewhere between pleasure and pain.

Slowly he draws his hands down the line of the corset, following the extreme curve of my altered body. As his fingers trail over my bottom and slip between my legs to the wet folds there, I close my eyes with a little sigh. He strokes me, pleasuring every inch of my skin.

My legs are incapable of holding me up so he gathers me in his arms and carries me to the bed, directing me to crawl into the centre on all fours. A plump cushion awaits me there, and flush with desire, I bend over it—my bottom raised invitingly.

The only sound is my breathing, the short little gasps and sighs he likes to hear as he keeps me waiting. The anticipation is sweet torment.

And now his hand connects with my right cheek—a sharp swat that makes me yelp. The bright flare of pain startles me, but by the time he smacks my other cheek, the pain shades into pleasure. I feel the flesh warming with each stroke, and as he spanks me, he comments on how my skin matches the color of the corset. I blush at both ends, whimpering and panting.

Breathless.

When the punishment finally stops, his fingers tease my tender flesh. I tremble beneath his touch, desperately wanting more attention. But I don't ask, not with my voice. I am a good little slave, sculpted by her master's hand, submissive and obedient—a statue brought to life.

Fabric rustles as he undresses, and now he is behind me on the bed, the warmth of his thighs against mine. He slides his hand between my legs, edging them apart. He teases me, his fingers moving in slow, lazy circles around my sex, brushing my clit and making me moan. I writhe, wriggling, begging him with my body to take me.

He doesn't make me wait long.

As the hardness of his cock presses against me, I close my eyes. He grips my tiny corseted waist and drives himself inside to fill me completely. Each thrust sends waves of excitement through me, and I cry out, surrendering fully.

He pushes himself into me, and my body is not mine to control. It's absolutely intoxicating—pounding, fucking hard—my upper body immobilized by the corset. I'm dizzy, both from my shallow bre athing and the pleasure he gives, a heady cocktail of sensations almost more than I can take.

But I want it all. And more.

The rising swell of ecstasy begins to consume us both. Climax overtakes me, and stars explode behind my eyes. By the time the throbbing bliss subsides, I'm blinded by tears of joy. My whole body is alive, euphoric, devastated.

But this isn't the end.

After confinement comes release.

The constriction gets me off, but there is a delicious duality to bondage. My master helps me to my feet. Unsteady and trembling, waves of pleasure bombard me. I stand before him. He turns me.

Panting and out of breath, I bend forward to grip the bedpost once more. He takes his time unlacing me. Freedom from the corset excites almost as much as the binding.

When the laces are loose enough, he unhooks the busk, opening the panels like a book. Air touches my skin, and I gasp. The full breath I take is another kind of bliss. He smiles, tracing the welts and indentations left by the corset's cruel bones. My skin is hypersensitive after the sensory deprivation, and his touch sends new waves of pleasure. My sex—reawakened and hungrier than ever— throbs in response.

He strokes my dewy slit, laughing softly at my predictable response. "Oh no," he says, "not yet."

I blush, squeezing my legs together. I am his to command, control, mold and shape.

Like a splash of blood, the red silk corset lies discarded on the bed. I curl into my master's arms. He has other corsets—some far more constricting than this one. Once my body recovers and the marks vanish from my skin, he will lace me into another and steal my breath again.

Freely, I give myself to him.

NASTY TO ME IS ALL ABOUT
SUPPORTING WHAT I
BELIEVE IN: PEOPLE'S RIGHT
TO DO WHAT THEY WANT
WITH THEIR BODIES AND
PLANNED PARENTHOOD,
NOW AND FOREVER!

CASSIE ALEXANDER

GALATEA

BY CASSIE ALEXANDER

*D*EAR COUSIN,
You wrote to ask how best to disburse my estate, whence comes my inevitable demise—and by my estate, I know you mean my statue, the queen of my collection, as you asked what her pedigree be. Likely you think of selling her to some museum, where she'll while away her days watching ignorant rubes pass by her.

As you and I have not seen each other in long years, and like as not ever again the way my cough is worsening, I will confess now to everything, for what have I to lose?

Confess—*and also beg.*

For if it is a curse to kiss cold lips, then cursed I fear I am.

You couldn't possibly understand. You liked your women lively, preening. I watched you watching them when we were younger, encouraging coy laughter—you had no appreciation of *silence*. You didn't understand the beauty of the becalmed pause, the eternal poise of quieted perfection.

But I, ever the connoisseur, did.

You appreciated the golden dew of youth, the lip's red-berry luster. The cheeks dusted pink as if by butterfly wing. I warned you those joys were fleeting. Couldn't you, learned man that you are, not look ahead and see their mothers, aunts, and spinster crones? What woman of forty maintains the glow of one but seventeen?

Women are fragile—their bodies meant to break and bend. So many would, without corsets, sway in a strong wind. And their minds? Don't get me started on their minds. Between the scholarly ones who cannot shut up and the ignorant ones unashamed of their ignorance—all of womankind can best be summed up by two rows of white teeth clicking, like a Spaniard's castanets, the sound so much the same.

To all this, when we were both much, much younger, I said, "No!"

So I found another way, which I will expound on here:

I imagined a perfect woman. Understand, such a thing was not possible outside the confines of the mind, at least not yet, but I pictured her entirely, every inch of her body.

Then, I found a perfect stone.

Pentelic marble is best. Heathens use stone from Italy, but Galatea was Greek, was she not? And I was in some small way courting Aphrodite.

After that, I began, with my block and my carving tools, to free the perfect woman trapped inside the marble.

Shall I tell you all of excavating my own? I think I shall. There needs be no shame at this late date.

I sensed her, waiting, like a chick hindered by too hard a shell, the hidden woman of my dreams. It took me months to carefully chisel the marble away, revealing her limbs piece by piece.

When I reached the edge of her brow, I kissed it. Marble ... heats up in a way that other minerals do not. It reflects your breath back to you. *It is the statue itself that breathes.* I doubted before, but now I know—I tasted how she longed to be free. All from one, pure kiss. (If you were to kiss a real woman, like as not, they would commence gabbing at you. Disgusting creatures! Feral sounds.)

And so, with a tormented heart, I carved her to the exclusion of all else. I forwent eating, sleeping, drinking wine—I would have torn her out of stone with my fingers if I could. I spent my days in a haze of chalky dust and my rare sleep in fevered dreams.

Soon, her face emerged, fully perfect, the same one from my fantasies. Her eyes were open wide, seeing all and pleading. I knew what she wanted, and I wanted that too—my lips met hers, closed, thick, and freshly hewn. I kissed away the dust still left upon them before I pulled back.

Here, at last, was a woman who would never talk, never change, and she was *mine*.

Days stretched into months. I made sure her hair was sculpted back so I could lick the delicate curve from shoulder to neck. In carving, the stone seemed to say one arm should reach out as if to meet me, so I carved it thus, tilting her hand so I could stroke it with my stubbled cheek. The other arm was by her side, of necessity, to hold whatever shimmering clothing I carved—in ancient times, women were forever getting into or coming out of ponds. I wanted no different for her. If any man were to see her, I wanted him to be jealous of my exceptional taste in antiquities, to think I had purchased her off the Parthenon's steps myself.

First one, then the other, and both her breasts were free. I will say, after that, I took a week off. Not to rest on my laurels, but because anytime I came into her chamber, they called to me. Their generous curves, and flawlessly placed nipples—I had never witnessed such perfection before and will not again until I see her once more. That week, I stood in front of her as if in prayer, leaning up to kiss them, where my worshipping continued.

After that, it was only a matter of time. Her back, graceful and strong, pulled from the marble easily. Her waist, tiny perfection, her belly, just the gentlest hint of a curve, and then her hips swelled outwards with one leg rising to take a step, freeing what was between her thighs and thence inside.

I carved that piece with quivering hands. I had come so far. And the portion of her I sought was within reach—I touched it, polished it with my callused fingertips. My loins, stirring more and more every day—I had to stroke myself on fleeting nights—swelled, pressing hard against the inside of my work pants.

I had not time to smooth everything—but was this not what I had waited for? I put my mouth against the space between her legs and kissed it fervently, pushing my tongue deep, readying the irregular texture of her grain with my spit—and I was upon her. I stood on my work chair so we were aligned, threw my apron aside, letting tools clatter to the ground. I freed myself— the weight of my love for her stiffening—and pushed myself inside my creation.

It hurt, but what consummation doesn't? And soon, it was perfect.

I had always known it would be.

I kissed her breasts, pressed her arm against my body. The smile of her lips studying, as she enjoyed my thrusts inside her. She would never not enjoy them, I realized—she couldn't change her mind. She alone would be beautiful and love me eternally.

The pure joy of complete acceptance—the likes of which I had never felt before—made me shout and grunt and finish myself inside her, slicking her with my heat, thrusting my softening organ in and out to stir it in her, just as if I had given my seed to a living woman—no, better, far better.

I will be honest. It took me a month to carve anything past that. What was the point?

Each time I reached my studio, I mounted my chair, and then

mounted her, finding her endlessly willing, endlessly satisfying. The heat of my body warmed her cool flesh, and I found every piece of her body absolute perfection. I took her three, four, five times a day, even found myself rising in the middle of the night to hurry down gas-lit corridors to be with her, like a sleepwalker fueled by desire.

But you, dear cousin, are a man of the Electrical Age, aren't you? You will never carve as I have carved, care as I have cared, nor love as I have loved. And what's worse, you're stuck with a wife and children.

I have slowed in my old age. The lust that once fueled me grows dim, but I cannot bear to be apart from her until the end.

And after that? *I beg of you. Do not sell her.* Take care of her. As I did, if you must. Was Tithonus ever worried about the happiness of his eternal Eos? If he wasn't, he should've been.

So love my goddess, please, as I loved her—but know she only dreams of me.

Your ever-loving,
Cousin

MASKS

BY 'NATHAN BURGOINE

*I*T'S THE FEEL OF HIS PALM WHEN WE SHAKE HANDS. There's a roughness, something off. Smiling through the introduction—though now I'm unsure this is an introduction—becomes the goal. Making the right noises.

Not like the noises I made last time.

Glasses of prosecco, discussions of guiding principles, designer suits, carefully coiffed men and women moving in ever-shifting circles of brief give-and-take conversations meant to offer promises of support while delicately ensuring most of the takes outweigh the gives.

The charity of the evening is like so many of the charities of this crowd—palatable, medical, offering a sense of self-congratulation—and the hors d'oeuvres are expensive.

I catch the man with the rough palm's name, and then excuse myself, shocked and suddenly aroused. I am hard. If anyone were to glance down, it would be obvious in this outfit, with no way to camouflage the bulge. Expensive suits are not up to that particular challenge.

So I leave and return to a bar where I can keep my back to the crowd while I calm down—though it takes far, far longer than it should. New glass in hand, I scan the crowd, have a heavy sip, and find the only person who can help me.

He nods as I approach, excuses himself from his small circle of socially elite do-gooders, and we clink glasses to say hello.

"Question. How many?" I ask.

There's only one thing I could be referring to, and it's not the first time I've asked, though it's definitely the first time I've asked in a surrounding as fine as this. I've never been convinced there was a reason to inquire among this particular crowd.

Foolish, it seems now, to assume I'd be the only one.

He takes a sip, raises his eyebrows in surprise, but scans room. I watch his eyes move, and when he sees the man with the roughness on his palm, his gaze catches hold.

"One," he says moments later, and pats my shoulder, moving off as though we've finished a conversation far less engaging than we have just concluded. We're not often seen together. My friend inhabits a circle or two lower than I do, and he is likely here as part of the organization, rather than a guest. It had been an unexpected surprise to see him.

Not as welcome as other surprises, of course.

One.

We used to be lovers, this friend and I, and still are in a fashion. He enjoys organizing. I enjoy his trust, which is the best thing we ever had between us, truth be told. Certainly, it is the most valuable.

I am caught twice more by small groups as I try to circle back to the man with the roughness on his palm. I know these groups see me as the worst sort of wealthy, a mix of new money and inheritance from the *wrong sort* of family. In some ways, it amuses me they find less discomfort with my queerness than with my history, but they no doubt assume I am the most transparent and nonthreatening sort of gay. Handsome in a suit, free with charitable donations, and a name to drop to others to accredit their open-minded liberalness. I enjoy a tiny smile at their expense.

If only they knew I was the *wrong sort* of queer, as well.

A few promises to get in touch, and an agreement some cause I can barely remember already, and I find myself with the man with the rough palm again, observing him among this third group of people.

There are other signs, perhaps. The width of his shoulders seems right, and this late into the evening I can see stubble on a chin he no doubt shaved before leaving his home. His nose is not quite even—a remnant of an accident, I wonder, or a fight? And his manners, though excellent, are just a shade facile.

He hasn't learned this game. Not like I have.

He keeps his palm closed, and I have to be careful not to stare, but finally, an opportunity comes to see him offer his hand to someone else—the endless introductions at these events are so tiresome.

Scars across his palm. A burn scar, I think, and wonder what happened.

"I assume you two have met?" says a forgettable man beside him, and I realize he is referring to myself and the man with the roughened palm.

"Yes," I say. *In mask and hood. Three weeks ago.* "Just earlier."

"I think you two have a lot in common."

"Do we?" the man with the roughened palm says.

"We do," I raise my glass. *You like to pinch with that hand, like to slap and twist, and I have had you inside me.* "Though I didn't think matchmaking was on the evening agenda."

48

The forgettable man blushes, titters, says he certainly wasn't intending anything like that, and he leaves us alone together by pretending to see someone who needs his attention. I can tell the man with the roughened palm enjoyed seeing him squirm. Yes, he's still new to this, moving in circles of people who are so very proper.

The others in our orbit move away, drawn by wealthier gravities, no doubt.

"Thank you," he says. "I had no idea how to get out of that conversation."

"Takes practice." *Perhaps you could tie them down next time. You enjoy nylon rope, no?*

"I'm not sure I'm up for it."

"The trick is to remind yourself it truly is for a good cause," I say. "But not to forget they all get as much out of it as the cause does. In this group, altruism is ego."

He laughs. It's a different laugh from the one conjured by someone twisting helplessly beneath his touch. That laugh was deeper, held the promise of things both withheld and to be blissfully endured.

I want him to know who I am. The realization is an icy shock, and for just a moment, it must show. He raises an eyebrow.

"Are you okay?"

That question has no place in an evening like this. He truly is new. Discomfort or awkward moments among these people are meant to be ignored until those who witnessed the embarrassments are alone and can eviscerate the one among them who dared slip up.

"I'm fine," I say. I finish my drink and place it on the passing tray of a waiter.

The man with the roughened palms smiles. "You've obviously had practice."

"I'm the worst sort of new money and wrong family," I say, and the enjoyment in the admission is profound. *I've been naked before this man already,* I think. *Why is honesty so thrilling now?*

It's no mystery, though. No hood. No mask.

This is very different kind of naked.

"I think I qualify as both as well. Anything you suggest?"

I love the way you fuck. "I'm sure you can take care of yourself, and anyone else who comes along."

Another laugh. "Are you quoting musicals at me?"

"Guilty." I shrug. "Though for appearance's sake, we should pretend it was an opera reference."

He nods, finishing his drink. He catches my eye, inhales, and manages a fairly adept placement as a tray floats past. He raises his hands, flashing that burn scar again without self-consciousness. Almost pride.

I want to feel that hand around my cock again. Now.

I shift my stance. The more I stare, the more confirmations of his identity appear. There are hairs exposed at the hollow of this throat, above the knot of his tie.

Before I can say anything else, we are joined by another small group. Shifting back into inanity, he doesn't meet my gaze through another round of pointlessness, and part of me wonders if he's doing so to avoid laughing.

Before we can be alone again, before I can think of a way to let him know what I know, someone touches my shoulder.

"Five minutes."

Damn. I need to start speaking soon.

I thank the organizer and turn back to the small group.

"I'm sorry, I need to step away," I say, and for the first time at one of these events, I'm sincere.

The others make noises meant to be disappointments.

The man with the roughened palm, however, regards me.

"I'd hoped ..." he says, but doesn't finish the sentence.

Inspiration strikes.

"Don't worry," I say. "You've left an impression already." There. His eyes leave mine, and he notices the way I'm holding my wrists, rubbing my thumbs on my forearms, right where nylon ropes burns—exquisite, joyful burns—faded over the last few weeks. A small tattoo. I'm usually so careful not to expose the graces inside of my left wrist.

There. In his eyes.

Recognition.

He swallows. "Well. I look forward to next time."

"Yes. You have my contact information, I believe."

I leave him there.

His suit trousers camouflage his erection no better than mine.

SPACE PUSSY!

BY MATTHEW F. AMATI

*T*OUCH MY PUSSY, SPACE FREAK, AND I promise I will jam that scalpel right up wherever your asshole might be located. Somewhere under those feathers, is my guess."

Earth Government had asked Mei-Hua Chen to travel with the Bno emissary and serve as Earth's first interstellar ambassador. A career diplomat, but also forty-something, divorced, and pretty much tired of people, Mei-Hua had agreed. She'd known it would involve sacrifices.

But this!

Her Bno contact, who went by the name Bno-ksh, fluttered its fronds. "Generative organs are on the alteration list. You must be surgically retrofitted before we take you into the Out There. Skin must be replaced with rad-proof lead mesh. You will need ozone-breathing lung sacs, crystalline oculoids to replace wet, fragile human eyes...."

"I get it, Bno. Squishy human bod, no good for space travel. You got to do what's necessary. But no slicers near my crotch, OK? The pussy stays. Once you remodel me, fucking will be the only fun I got left."

"If you'll pardon my saying so, *the human* has no idea what fucking truly is."

"You take that back right now, feather-face!"

"When we replace your primitive human organ with a four-pronged, six-socketed Genitron 4000, the human will know fucking more profoundly satisfying than it could ever have imagined!"

"Four prongs? Six sockets? Who'll want to bork me with that get-up between my legs?"

Bno-ksh gestured skyward. "There's a whole universe out there, human."

Well, as long as EarthGov was footing the bill. Mei-Hua shrugged and laid herself down on the soft blue slab. Darkness closed in.

When she awoke, the Bno ship was halfway to Proxima Centauri. And Mei-Hua was changed, changed utterly.

Her skin was sable silk, impervious to the worst particles a boiling sun could spew. Her eyes were crystals; her lungs breathed ozone; her heart was a perfectly efficient dynamo pumping blue fluid.

And down *there...*

"Now the human is ready to see the stars," Bno-ksh said.

"What *is* this thing?" came Mei-Hua's newly synthetic voice. Hyper-articulated fingers explored the novel equipment between her legs.

"It is recommended you read the manual." Bno-ksh tossed Mei-Hua a five-pound binder crammed with tiny text and diagrams.

"Instructions for my space pussy, eh?" Mei-Hua flipped the pages.

"Frottage dial settings. Nerve sensitivity algorithms. Orgasmulator calibrations. Holy cats, this thing is two thousand pages!"

"Think of it as moving from remedial fucking to the Ph.D. level, human. Some hard study will be required of you."

On Korvax Prime, Mei-Hua reeled, as new interstellar travelers do, to see the thousands of species crowding the narrow streets under ammonia rain and flickering xenon signs. Her newly-indestructible eye checked out insectoids, squid-like hulks, delicate sashaying tulip-beings, hideous muck-heaps leaving slime trails, and even a few almost-human things here and there.

The first day was difficult. Paperwork and more paperwork. *You are the diplomatic attaché from where? Never heard of "Urth", I'm afraid.* And *sign this,* and *wait for that,* and sit through yet another meeting.

As the three suns were setting and the nightlife of Korvax got underway, Mei-Hua said, "Let's try it."

"Pardon?"

"The Genitro-whaddayacallit. The Space Pussy. Let's give it a whirl."

"Very well. The infrared-light district is this way. The fleshpots of an inter-reaches hubworld are yours for the exploring. I assume your government is paying the expenses for this ... er ..."

"—research. Let's call it research."

Under a blinking depiction of ovipositors, the proprietor of Xthi's Bespoke Intimacies handed Mei-Hua a form. Mei-Hua blinked.

"Help me with this, Bno-ksh. It's in chicken scratches."

"It's a consent form."

"Oh, I consent. I do."

"Caution advised. Some species enjoy being devoured in the act of coitus. Others like it when their lover lays parasitic eggs in their wounds. Still, others like to consume Rakkaplangian spermatophores. If a beachball-sized blob of cockroach semen sounds appetizing ..."

"OK, ok. None of those things, please."

"They're bound to think you a prude, you know." The Bno filled out the form on Mei-Hua's behalf.

The madam said, "We've chosen the perfect lover for an interspecies beginner. Meet Xrjjchthxxx, an arachnon from Tantalus IV."

From behind a curtain stepped a hellish apparition forged in Mei-Hua's skeeviest nightmares. She wasn't ... but she *was* ... looking at an eight-eyed, blue-furred spider the size of a Great Dane.

Merely finding that thing in her bathtub would have given Mei-Hua the screaming oopizootics. And she was supposed to ...

Bno-ksh said, "You'll never get laid with that attitude. Oh, dear, you haven't adjusted your inhibition dampers, have you?"

"My what-whats?" Mei-Hua was keeping a wary eye on the spider.

"It's in the manual. Set your inhibitions too high and you'll turn down Don Juan. Too low and you'll be humping the furniture. Here, allow me." Bno-Ksh fiddled with a remote.

And Mei-Hua's steel knees turned to butter.

That eight-legged spidey-stud was *gorgeous*.

Bristly, blue legs caressed Mei-Hua's metal skin. Opaque arachnid eyelets peered into her eyes. From a flap on the spider's abdomen, two glistening prongs emerged, quivering with heat.

"TWO dongs? What do I do with ..." But Mei-Hua had forgotten; her Space Pussy came with an array of receptacles. There were plenty of options.

Mei-Hua squawked as the arachnon's twin penises entered Port #2 and Port #4 of her Genitron 4000. The spider moved tenderly in and out of her. The Genitron 4000 hummed and clicked, consulting memory banks that contained pleasuring data on millions of species. It extruded a tentacle that massaged a white sticky patch on the arachnon's thorax. The spider's legs trembled. It emitted a high-pitched *eek-eek-eek* sound.

The universe folded itself inside out. Reality exploded deep within Mei-Hua. The arachnon gave a final thrust, and Mei-Hua passed through nine non-Euclidian dimensions and fourteen Riemann topologies before curling up on the floor in a sizzling post-coital trance.

"Satisfied?" Bno asked.

Weakly, Mei-Hua replied, "Just getting started."

So began a galactic odyssey for her newly-retrofitted human body. She learned the wiles of male, female, unmale, nomale, trigender, omnisex, uniperv, kemmerer, quartch, Lobzian, and aloof. She canoodled with the bio-curious, the herma-adono-aphroditic, the meiosis-manic, the anaerobic, and the pervatomic. She connected with bear-men, cat-women, tentacled abominations, hulking hawkanthropes, and slender green triffidons.

Diplomatic duties seemed dull and distant. "Human, should we attend the Conference of Class-M Waterworlds?"

"Nah, let's see if the rock giants of Magnar are feeling frisky today."

She got into sauropod swinging, slime-squatting, frond-felching, and communal telepathic orgies involving millions of beings. And sublight sucking, and sentient feces-fetish, and spacetime vector bondage, and de-evolution kink and amoeba tickling and Tribonian triple-tongue action and Rigellian gland-gunk, and of course, volcano play.

Mei-Hua subbed herself to a legion of lizard soldiers, letting them use her. She was glad that the play never got out of hand because the safe word was somewhere on the ultrasonic spectrum. The Genitron 4000 spewed forth a vat of "eggs," and the moaning Kh'thrikk mercenaries uncovered their cloacas and sprayed the deposit with hot milt.

More business to ignore. "You've got orders to meet with the Emissary of Evermore, a ten-million-year-old energy emperor."

"And miss the nitrogen pudding baths of Bellatrix? No way!" Roleplaying as Dom-monarch of the Horsecock Nebula, Mei-Hua made groveling worm-beings service her, employing their entire limbless bodies as pleasure-prongs.

She even got it on with Bno-ksh itself, and though it was dull in the sack, she was amused to find out her mentor had four vaginas.

"Ready for the big time?" Bno-ksh asked as the ship sped toward a diplomatic confab they had already missed.

"Big? How big?"

At the far end of the Universe, before the towering columns of glowing gas known as the Pillars of Creation, a glow appeared, so intense even Mei-Hua's crystalline eyes couldn't comprehend it. A deep voice resounded in her psyche, and she was overcome with a profound peace—a peace that passed all understanding.

Mei-Hua gasped. "Am I going to diddle ... *God?*"

Afterward, glowing with pleasure, Mei-Hua had to admit the Big Guy had been pretty good.

Then the fun ended. EarthGov called. They were pissed.

The Earth Government charged Mei-Hua with serious dereliction of duty. Their Ambassador had failed to establish consulates on the most important worlds—had not, in fact, established a single embassy anywhere. She had not contacted any of the potentates on her list, had not forged relationships with the Kargon or Slurpsid Empires.

"Have you even made contact with the Pinniped Panjandrum of Gliese 887-A?"

Mei-Hua ransacked her memory. "That dishy walrus king? I mean, yes. I did make contact. In a sense." Thinking back, a shiver of pleasure ran through her. Those whiskers!

"At least, fulfill your PR responsibilities. The people of Earth desire a statement from their Ambassador. How would you characterize your experience among ancient and mighty interstellar civilizations thus far?"

Mei-Hua answered quickly and enthusiastically. *"Fucking amazing!"*

She thought for a moment, then added:

"And vice versa."

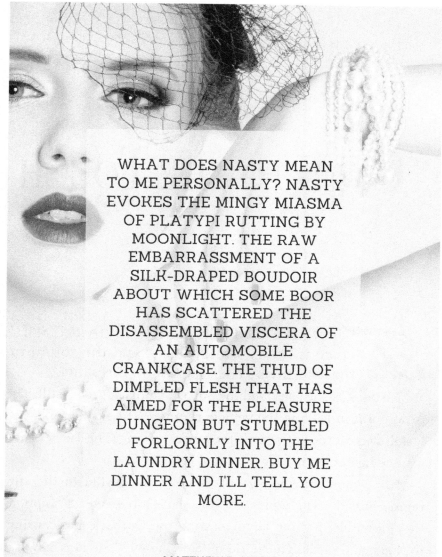

WHAT DOES NASTY MEAN TO ME PERSONALLY? NASTY EVOKES THE MINGY MIASMA OF PLATYPI RUTTING BY MOONLIGHT. THE RAW EMBARRASSMENT OF A SILK-DRAPED BOUDOIR ABOUT WHICH SOME BOOR HAS SCATTERED THE DISASSEMBLED VISCERA OF AN AUTOMOBILE CRANKCASE. THE THUD OF DIMPLED FLESH THAT HAS AIMED FOR THE PLEASURE DUNGEON BUT STUMBLED FORLORNLY INTO THE LAUNDRY DINNER. BUY ME DINNER AND I'LL TELL YOU MORE.

MATTHEW F. AMATI

COLD TO THE TOUCH

BY TIM WAGGONER

*T*URN OFF THE ENGINE," CELIA SAYS. HER voice is husky with arousal, and the sound of it makes Travis's cock harden in his pants.

He does as she asks, and the Subaru Outback grows still. There is no point in leaving the vehicle running. The heater isn't on. In fact, it was off the entire time they were driving. The Turners never use the heater, no matter how cold it is out.

For a moment, the two of them sit and listen to the storm raging outside. The winds are hurricane force, over 80 mph, and they howl like a thing alive, blasting the Outback and causing it to shake and rattle. The world outside the windshield is a swirling maelstrom of snow, and all they can see is white. They are parked on an out-of-the-way country road, but from their surroundings, they could just as easily be in Antarctica. It's as if a new Ice Age has arrived, wiping out humanity and leaving Travis and Celia the only two people left. It's the strongest blizzard in the last fifty years, the weather forecasters warned, maybe in the last century. A state of emergency has been declared, and the road conditions are so appallingly dangerous that all travel—except for police cars, fire trucks, and ambulances—is prohibited. But that didn't stop Travis and Celia. If anything, the danger only encouraged them more.

Travis turns to his wife and sees that she's already pulling off her sweater. Celia isn't wearing a bra, and as her breasts slip free from the fabric, Travis reaches out and brushes his fingers across the left one. She closes her eyes, gives a small smile, and shudders. Her flesh is cool to the touch, her nipple dark and hard as marble. His cock swells to the point where it becomes painful, and he draws in a hissing breath. Celia pulls her sweater the rest of the way off and tosses it to the floor. Her gaze drops to his crotch, and she reaches out and gently rubs the bulge in his jeans. Travis moans and squeezes her breast. Now it's Celia's turn to moan as he takes her nipple between his cold thumb and forefinger and rolls it back and forth.

The cold has the paradoxical effect of numbing flesh while at the same time intensifying physical sensation. Travis doesn't know why this is; he only knows that it turns him on and that it has the same effect on Celia. Every touch is cold fire, every kiss a small, frigid bite.

Celia draws down his zipper, pulls his cock free and then—after leaning over to blow cool air over it—takes it in her mouth. After the cold, the sensation of wet warmth comes as a shock to Travis, and he nearly explodes in Celia's mouth. But he takes in a deep breath of the cold air in the vehicle, and as its coolness settles in his lungs, he feels himself pull back from the edge. That's another thing about the cold: it slows things down, forces you to take your time. In many ways, this is what Travis likes most about it.

That Travis and Celia met each other was something of a miracle. It's difficult enough for people to find a partner they're sexually compatible with under normal circumstances. But when you have a more ... *specialized* sexual need, one that most people have never heard of, it isn't merely difficult to find a match. It's damn near impossible. And if your particular kink is rare enough, even the almighty Internet isn't much help. They are plenty of sites that claim to help you find sex partners, and Travis tried more than a few, but without any luck. He tried to make do, keeping the thermostat set low whenever he brought a woman back to his apartment, cracking the bedroom window in winter. Most women he dated despised the cold, especially when they were naked, and as for the few who didn't mind it, they didn't share his passion—his absolute, soul-gnawing need—to fuck in the cold.

But then, just when he'd given up hope of ever being truly fulfilled, he met Celia. He was waiting for a cab outside the building where his law office was located. It was late January and bitterly cold out. The wind came at him sideways, and it felt like blades of ice cutting into his exposed flesh. He grew erect almost immediately. And then Celia came out of the building and stepped onto the sidewalk. Despite the weather, she wore a short skirt, the thinnest of jackets, and—this should've tipped him off right away—open-toed shoes. He would find out later that she was an oral surgeon whose practice was in the building, and she'd come out to wait for a friend who was picking her up for lunch.

Travis checked her out. She turned to look at him. He smiled. She smiled back. And then her gaze dropped to his crotch, and her smile widened.

"Do you always get a hard-on when it's cold?" she asked. There was no mockery in her tone. Instead, she sounded almost hopeful.

"Always," he said truthfully.

Celia looked at him for a moment before reaching her left hand up her skirt. She removed her skirt and stepped close to him. She raised her wet fingers to his face, he inhaled her heady musk for the first time—her scent reminding him of sex on cold, crisp winter mornings—and he knew he'd never be alone again.

They married less than a year later, and things were good between them. They ran the air conditioning in their home—on the coldest setting—all year long, and each winter they kept an eye on the forecast, and when it was cold enough, they went outside and fucked until they couldn't feel their bodies anymore. When the forecasters announced that the winter storm of the century was approaching, they knew that they had to take advantage of the opportunity, for it would never come again in their lifetime.

So here they were, in the middle of a deadly nor'easter, and they'd never been so turned on in their lives.

It takes only seconds for them to remove the rest of their clothes, and then they climb in the back where they'll have more room. Travis's skin tingles almost painfully in the frigid air as if thousands of electric needles strike his flesh. And then Celia is in his arms, kissing him, her fingernails digging into his shoulders hard enough to draw blood. They lose themselves in each other, and even though their bodies are long-familiar and well-traveled landscapes, with the blizzard of all blizzards roaring outside, hurricane-force winds buffeting the Outback, everything feels new, their bodies suddenly uncharted territory. The sensation is so intense, so all-consuming, that it's transcendent.

They fuck in every position they can manage given the space, and there is no inch of skin left untouched. Celia comes before he does, her vaginal walls contracting around his cock, the muscles spasming and rippling until he can hold back no longer, and releases inside her. It feels as if he's filling her with his very essence, losing himself in her in the most profound and literal sense.

They collapse against each other, breath coming in ragged gasps, sweat coating their skin like liquid ice. Before long they're shivering, as much from the aftereffects of the sex as from the cold.

"That was amazing," Celia says.

"The best," Travis agrees.

"It'll never be this good again, will it?" Her tone is wistful. "How can it be? There will never be another storm like this, will there? Not for us."

Travis knows she's right.

They don't discuss any further. They don't have to. They sit up, and Travis opens the Outback's side door. Cold wind blasts into the vehicle's interior, flinging snow and ice at them. He takes Celia's hand and together, naked, they step outside and begin walking away from the Outback.

It's five days before snow removal crews get to the back roads, and that's when the Outback is discovered. When state troopers arrive to check it out, it doesn't take them long to find Travis and Celia's frozen bodies in a nearby snowdrift. They made it less than twenty feet from the vehicle before collapsing.

It's snowing that day, not hard, and there's a gentle wind that sometimes kicks up a half-hearted gust before dying back down. During one of these gusts, a trooper thinks he hears the sound of a man and woman laughing with unbridled joy, but he tells himself that it's only his imagination, and the snow continues to fall.

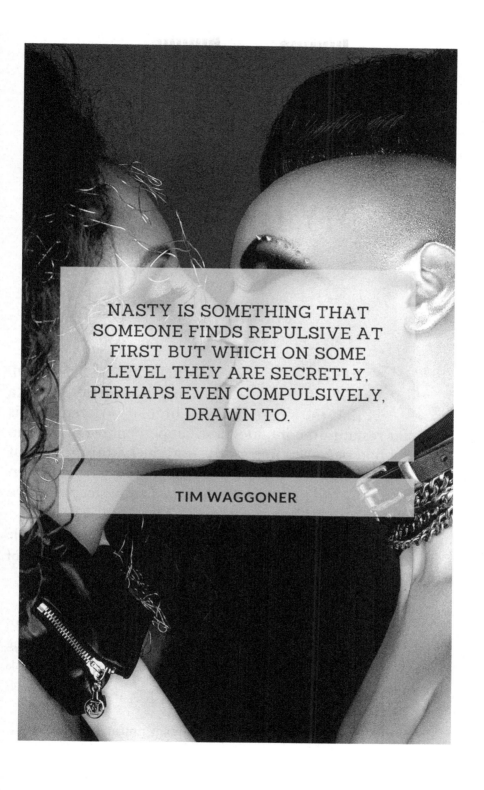

NASTY IS SOMETHING THAT
SOMEONE FINDS REPULSIVE AT
FIRST BUT WHICH ON SOME
LEVEL THEY ARE SECRETLY,
PERHAPS EVEN COMPULSIVELY,
DRAWN TO.

TIM WAGGONER

My Best Dish

I RECEIVED AN IMMENSE AMOUNT OF PLEASURE TELLING my boyfriend Mayetta that the vegan hot dog he had ordered at this hipster restaurant contained a small percentage of human DNA. I had been waiting, giddy, until he had finished half the faux wiener. Over the weekend, while rereading an old lexicon, I fell in love with the word epicaricacy; I once hoped to score 800 on the verbal portion of the SAT.

Mayetta dropped the remains of the hot dog on the recyclable paper plate. He stared at his fingertips, covered in a few crumbs of gluten-free roll grilled alongside the hot dog.

"Does not," he said.

"A recent food science study found that two percent of hot dogs sold tested positive for human DNA. The most damning results were in so-called vegetarian dogs. I think it was two-thirds or three-fourths or some ridiculous number."

"You're making this up."

"Would I?" I lifted up my vegan weiner, untouched until now.

66

It had cooled to a tepid temperature, but I dunked most of it into my cup of water, saturating the bun, and shoved the entire thing into my mouth. My cheeked puffed, my gag reflux threatened, but I chewed and chewed as Mayetta's face became a Dorian Gray print, ugly with disgust.

"It's how the gurgitators eat," I said with a mouth full. "You've never watched the Nathan's Hot Dog Eating Contest? The Wingbowl? That's a Philly tradition." Bits of human-tainted, dyed soy and soaked bun, dissolving before our eyes thanks to my saliva, flew from my mouth like I was a gorging dragon.

My prince scooted back on his chair, metal scraped against the tile and disturbed the surrounding hipster snackers. He could have made a futile gesture of leaving the restaurant, but I had driven us, and it was a long walk to his home.

I gulped from the cup I'd dunked the hot dog in to clear my mouth.

"The real question, what I really want to know, is the source of the DNA," I said. "Not the person, but what *part* of the person."

"It's still better than eating a real hot dog. The World Health Organization has classified those as dangerous as tobacco and asbestos. Think about that. Asbestos. In your mouth, a clump of toxins creeping down your throat until it sits in your stomach. Dead meat in your belly. Whether it starts rotting first—because all the preservatives make digestion take days—or your stomach acid breaks it down into its component parts, those cancerous fibers are going to paint your colon with melanoma black."

"You've been inside my colon, did the tip of your dick turn black?"

He shook a finger at me. "Rectum. Just behind the sphincter is *your rectum.*"

His father taught medicine. His mother worked as a nurse.

Mayetta had a small scar along his torso from an appendectomy. I wondered who cut him open ....

I adored the scene in *Jaws* where the men bond by comparing scars. Cicatrix is another SAT word.

"Perhaps if your skin was browner, you'd have a bigger dick and reach my colon." He's the brownest boy I'd ever fucked. I'm pink, like pork, the other white meat.

Mayetta tugged at the tiny hairs on his chin. They curled and bristled. "And the racist joke happens while we're still eating and not on the ride home. A new record."

I shrugged. "It's no fun to make when we're alone."

"How about a Muslim joke? That would be appreciated. Everyone in America likes those."

I take hold of his hand, my index finger tapping the spot on the wrist where a paramedic would check for the pulse. "I love you. Like Lawrence of Arabia loved those boys," I said.

"You told me Lawrence of Arabia was raped by the Turks which left him with ... issues."

"Rape, bigotry, cannibalism, I think we're covering so many taboos and it's not even two p.m. Do I win Boyfriend-of-the-Year award?"

"Only if you pay for lunch."

He sighed. "Extortion. I do love you."

Mayetta leaned over to accost the nearest diner, a woman with long hair that showed strata of dyeing, dark and dusty at the ends close to the floor, faded as it Rapunzeled up to salt-and-pepper by her scalp. Her shapeless dress also could not decide on just one or two colors, but assaulted the visible spectrum.

"So, this guy sitting across from me—I just met him on Grindr this morning—tells me that vegan dogs have human DNA in them. I'm wondering if the workers at the vegan dog factory spit into the tofu vats or ..."

The woman wiped her lips with a napkin that already showed a great deal of lipstick. "You swallow three spiders over a lifetime of sleep, so even if a waiter spits in your food, it can't be worse than that."

Mayetta laughed. "You do not swallow spiders—"

The man across from her, who might have been her son, might have been her younger brother, could have been a boyfriend (good for her!) had an upper lip of cappuccino foam. "It's true. I've caught a spider in the house and dropped it onto Astra's lips while she dreamed. I had to push it a little with my fingers but inside it went. And she swallowed. She swallows everything."

"Lucky you," I said. "My boy spits. Though I suppose some of my DNA has to make its way into his gullet."

When Mayetta frowned, he denied me his beautiful teeth. Not a single cavity, whereas my mouth could set off a metal detector. "The Quran forbids cannibalism."

"Sodomy, too. I would imagine sodomizing a Jew would annoy Allah even more."

"You'll so endear yourself to my family with that line."

Mayetta stood up. I pushed my chair back an inch from the wooden table. He walked around until he stood behind my wheelchair. He leaned down and whispered into my ear. "Of course, ghuls are part of Allah's design. Islam means—"

"Voluntary submission to God." I spoke softly, only for him.

The first time he went down on me had been the first time he'd ever taken a dick in his mouth. His beautiful teeth scraped the tender skin, especially around my circumcision mark. But I didn't complain: watching his handsome face engulf me, left me swooning even as he scratched my glans. I felt as if he were shaving bits of me, swallowing them first before I quickly came.

And now be bit down on the lobe of my ear. His incisors piercing the lump of skin. I shuddered at the pain and thought of our first night together in bed ... then remembered seventh grade, when my next door neighbor, a younger boy who had a lazy eye tried to pierce my ear with a sewing needle, a lighter and a block of ice. He had caught a drop of my blood on his thumb and stuck it in his mouth.

I came up with a song I'd croon in my head:

Little Danny Horner

Sat in the corner,

Only ten and cross-eye

He found on his thumb,

Blood to spell redrum

And said 'Why do you have a wet fly?'

All the hipsters in the place smiled at us. How kind of this brown-skinned fag to be helping his boyfriend, missing both legs beneath the knee but with an undeniable erection in the crotch of his worn jeans, out of the restaurant: they must be going home after sharing a nice meal.

We were going home where I would share the nicest meal I could make.

LIBRARY DUST

BY ROBERT BROUHARD

THE SNEEZE ECHOED IN THE SMALL LIBRARY and caused an electric shock that ended at the tip of his cock. His eyes darted around the room to find the source. Again, another burst came from the stacks.

"Ungh." Vince barely stifled the sound.

The knowledge that the dusty tomes would bring out the best allergies in people might be why, deep down, he chose to be a librarian in the first place. The thrill of sneezing—anyone's sneezing—excited him into a frenzy.

Another explosive sneeze. He gripped the desk with one hand as he continued checking out old Mrs. Freeman's stack of gardening books with the other. *Beep.* Someday soon, she'll have checked out the whole section.

"Sounds like someone might be getting a cold," Mrs. Freeman's gravelly voice said. She must have taken the look on Vince's face to be concern. *Beep.*

Another spurt of sound from the middle of the library.

71

"Oh!" Vince thrust his groin against the countertop in front of him. Grinding against it. *They're multiple, just like her...* He stopped his thought. *Just like who? Who was that?*

Another sneeze followed by one more in quick succession broke his thought, and his hips jerked, grinding hard against the counter. *Rose! It was Mrs. Rose.* His mind flashed. When he was younger, she had always worn those low halter tops that showed so much. And when she'd had a sneezing attack, it had been anything goes. Until that one day when—*Achoo*, pop! He had seen everything.

Oh, Mrs. Rose.

Vince's thoughts stopped his hands for a bit until Mrs. Freeman cleared her throat. "Oh, sorry, Mrs. Freeman," he managed. His tumescence eagerly begged for more attention as he scanned another book while glancing over her grey curls. *Beep.*

Mrs. Freeman pushed her stack closer to Vince so he wouldn't have to reach as far forward. A sneeze rang out like a crashing wave. His eyes locked on Mrs. Freeman's. The pure, joyous sensation must have been clear in his eyes. *She must see it.* His tightly encased cock ground against the counter. Another joyous sneeze. His lips parted, and the gasp of air would have been audible to anyone else around, but only Mrs. Freeman was here. Yet another sneeze. "Fu—" was all he could say as he thrust into the counter. He pushed against it, but the echo died down. The sneezing had stopped.

"Are you feeling all right?"

Vince regained enough composure to start pulling more books across the infrared scanner. *Beep. Beep.*

"I'm ... I'm fine, Mrs. Freeman," Vince managed.

Who had sneezed? He looked past Mrs. Freeman into the stacks of books. Only two or three people were visible, which was normal for this time of day. It typically wasn't busy in the early afternoons on a Tuesday, usually just single mothers and some random other people. So little activity in fact, that Vince was the only one watching the check-out counter. The other librarians, Laura and Willa, were shelving books.

Maybe he didn't really care who it was.

No, their sneezes were enthralling. He secretly hoped the book dust in the air would make them restart. Or maybe he could sneak off into the bathroom for a couple of minutes and relieve his built-up need to come. *Beep.*

Vince continued pressing himself into the counter as thoughts of those bursting sneezes filled his brain.

Definitely going into the bathroom as soon as I finish with Mrs. Freeman.

Beep.

Mr. Freeman walked slowly up to his wife, his cane ticking on the tile as he left the carpeted area where the stacks were. He put two books on top of Mrs. Freeman's dwindling pile. The light above the counter shone of his balding head. "Dearie, I found the other John Brookes book you were looking for and another that looked interesting. Sorry I was delayed for a bit." Mr. Freeman's British accent flowed out like silk. *Beep.*

"Thank you!" Mrs. Freeman said with a growing smile.

"Oh. Dearie, do you have a ti ... a ti ..." Mr. Freeman's sudden sneeze shocked Vince and Mrs. Freeman.

Vince's eyes popped wide as he watched Mr. Freeman's face contort as another sneeze built up. It issued with explosive force. To the thrill of Vince, Mr. Freeman didn't even try to cover it. Vince gasped and had no control as his hands went below the counter, rubbing, massaging, urging his cock. Then another sneeze issued.

"Oh!" Vince gasped loudly.

And another sneeze shattered the air. Mr. Freeman's face looked anguished.

Mrs. Freeman's face looked concerned, but no one was looking at her.

Vince's face was full of passion and urgency. He rubbed himself. He had no cares about anything but the pleasure he felt in the audio and visual experience before him.

"Are you okay, honey?" Mrs. Freeman asked, her hand rubbing her husband's shoulder.

"I ..." *Achoo* was all he could respond.

Vince's ragged breathing was getting louder. He unzipped his pants and took out his cock. He grasped it. Thrusting it wildly into his circled fist, he watched Mr. Freeman's face contort and twitch.

Mr. Freeman's breath caught. Hitched. Shuddered. Stopped. Normalized. Caught. And ...

Vince felt it coming. He felt his desire to come flow forward. He grabbed the book that was on top of Mrs. Freeman's stack, *Small Gardens* by John Brookes.

Mr. Freeman let out a succession of sneezes that didn't seem like they would stop for years.

Boom.

Boom.

Boom

Boom.

BOOM.

Vince ejaculated into the book at a random middle section. Each squirt in unison with the sneezes, the orgasm's waves were beautiful because Mr. Freeman's sneezes were. It was the best mind-shattering orgasm Vince could remember or he believed he would ever have. Mr. Freeman let out one last sneeze, blew his nose in a tissue Mrs. Freeman finally fished out of her purse, and said, "Excuse me. So sorry. I think I'm coming down with a cold."

Vince couldn't find his voice to speak back for a bit. He just shook his head and nodded in a roundabout way.

Vince looked down at the mess he made in the "Narrow Spaces" chapter of the book and closed it. He placed *Small Gardens* into

Mrs. Freeman's checked-out pile. Muscle memory took over and the remaining three books were passed by the scanner. *Beep. Beep. Beep.*

He didn't bother to zip up. No one could see below his upper belly anyway.

He waved and managed a "Pleasant reading!" as Mr. and Mrs. Freeman went through the anti-theft scanners, a loud beeping alerting the few people who were in the library. Vince's eyes widened, and he waved his hand for the Freemans to just keep going.

They did.

Vince adjusted himself and zipped up his pants. The clouds were slowly clearing from his brain.

Did I scan that John Brookes book out to them? was the first thought that came to him after his brain restarted.

Someone was standing at the counter. Vince looked up. A man with a very flushed face held a stack of books. Vince recognized him as a weekly regular who was usually there during busier times, Charles Willis.

Keeping his eyes downcast, Charles hefted his books onto the counter. Vince recognized the names on the books as they were some of his favorites too: Susie Bright, Anaïs Nin, Kilt Kilpatrick, and more. He also understood Charles' embarrassment.

Vince skipped the small talk, took Charles' library card, and scanned it into the computer to bring up his account. *Beep.* Nothing overdue. Vince grabbed the first book, one of the *Herotica* series. *Beep.*

A sneeze echoed. Vince noticed Charles' head snap up and look toward the stacks. Another sneeze. Charles inhaled sharply before a shuddering issued from between his lips.

And just like that, the sneezing stopped.

Charles slowly turned back to the counter. His eyes met

Vince's. Vince smiled warmly at him, and Charles smiled back. That sharing of understanding smiles was more real than anything either had felt in a long time.

The moment was broken by another sneeze that thrilled them both.

HE IS VERY PROUD THAT THIS
ANTHOLOGY IS GIVING A
PORTION OF ITS PROFITS TO
PLANNED PARENTHOOD (AS
SOON AS HE LEARNED THAT, HE
HAD TO SUBMIT TO IT).

ROBERT BROUHARD

THE DESPERATE FLESH

BY KELLY ROBSON

*T*HE KAREN KAIN CENTRE FOR CONVALESCENT CARE WAS GENEROUSLY ENDOWED, rumor said, by a bisexual Rosedale matron who'd nursed a lifelong crush on the prima ballerina. When Margaret took the job as director, she tried to find out the mysterious benefactor's identity. Not to out her, of course, or even to share the juicy gossip among her friends, but to satisfy her burning curiosity. No go, though. The secret was buried under a tangle of trusts and numbered companies, and Margaret had too much work on her plate to keep digging.

She'd expected to be busy in her new job, but she hadn't expected to face a scandal right away—and certainly not one that included flashing both geriatric and barely-legal flesh in the accessible seats in the opera house's dress circle, in front of thousands of white-haired opera-fans.

The posters on Margaret's wall rattled as Betty and Pia shut the office door behind them. The black and white portrait of Karen

Kain stared down from the back wall—strength, grace, power, and flexibility encapsulated in one simple gesture, a pair of hands laid on a flawless cheek as if in prayer. If anyone could help Margaret get through this day with dignity, it was her.

Saint Karen Kain, help me now, Margaret thought. She took a deep breath and turned to face her two employees.

"The last time I checked, the opera house wasn't a nudist colony." Margaret tried to sound calm and graceful, keep her movements controlled yet relaxed, just like a ballerina's. "Do you want to explain what happened?"

"Serena can move fast when she wants to," said Pia.

"We couldn't do anything," said Betty. "The overture was already playing."

"You couldn't disturb the performance," Margaret said. The two women nodded. "So I suppose your clothes just fell off, Betty?"

Betty raked her fingers through her thick pink hair. "I didn't want Serena to be the only one showing skin."

"Really? Because it seems like you came prepared."

Betty pulled down the collar of her cowgirl-patterned scrubs to reveal a scarlet sequin pasty complete with a dangling tassel. Margaret winced as the sequins gleamed in the light of the overhead fluorescents. Wearing a costume piece under scrubs didn't do any harm, but it was so trashy. So tasteless.

"Just a coincidence." Betty tugged the tassel. "I'm trying out a new adhesive."

"So you weren't planning to strip during the opera?"

"It wasn't a tease. It was just nudity. I could show you the difference—"

"No." Margaret lurched to her feet. She steadied herself on her desk, tried to make the movement look natural. "I can't believe I have to say this, Betty. No stripping when you're on the clock. None."

Betty rolled her eyes. "Being naked isn't stripping. There's a difference."

Margaret stole a glance at the gorgeous calm form on the poster behind her, that paragon of strength and femininity, muscles sheathed in flawless flesh, and costumed in perfect harmony with taste and tradition. When she turned back to her employees, she tried to look generous, yet imperious.

"That's enough," she said, "you can go."

Betty slipped out. Pia lingered in the doorway.

"I don't blame you," Margaret said in a hushed voice. "Supervising staff isn't your responsibility."

Pia fingered her crucifix. "This isn't going to stop," she said.

It would have to stop, Margaret thought. Her entire career depended on it.

><><

Karen Kain's mission was to house and care for Toronto's geriatric lesbian population. With only eighteen beds in a compact heritage mansion on the corner of Queen and University, Karen could hardly house them all, but the city also had Ivan Coyote House, a hundred-bed long-term care home on Church and King. Together, Karen and Ivan were the bulwark against scattering women to the far edges of the city to live side-by-side with old men who sprung semis when they heard the word lesbian.

The next incident happened at City Hall, just a few days later. When Margaret got the call, she peeled out the door, ran full out for three blocks, and staggered through Nathan Philips Square with a vicious stitch in her side. Out of shape; out of control. Once, Margaret had been a young dancer. Tireless, dedicated, unflappable. Now she was a mess. A mess in charge of a mess.

Margo, Titus, and Trinh sat on folding chairs in a quiet corner of the City Hall lobby, clothes crumpled underfoot, gray wool blankets draped over their bare shoulders. Betty stood beside them—clothed, thank goodness. A few steps away, Pia flirted in Spanish with a tall police officer whose duty belt fit snugly around ample hips. Pia's navy blue scrubs were the exact shade of the officer's uniform.

"I don't think there'll be a problem," Betty whispered to Margaret. "That cop is on our side."

"Mmm," said Titus. "Sure is."

Margo grinned and shrugged the blanket off her shoulders. A ray of sunlight highlighted her plummy areolas. Trinh dropped her blanket too. Margaret snatched the blankets from the floor, fumbled them, folded them into bulky wads. When she finished, she placed them across the two women's laps, covering their spare gray bushes. It wasn't much, but it would have to do. Titus lifted herself creakily from her chair, drew her blanket from beneath her butt, folded it herself, and settled back down with the fabric neatly draped across her bony thighs.

The officer glanced over, adjusted her sunglasses, and turned her attention back to Pia.

The elevator dinged. The general manager of Long-Term Care pushed through the parting doors and stalked across the lobby, glaring at Margaret as he adjusted the already-perfect knot in his tie.

"The police might be on our side," said Margaret. "But the city isn't."

The city had never been on Karen Kain's side. They wanted the building for a museum, maybe a cultural center, anything but an old-age home for lesbians. Margaret's job was to change the city's mind.

〜 ⁹ 〜

Ivan Coyote House was a charmless brutalist structure from the

1960s; four stories on a quarter block of downtown real estate dwarfed by steel-and-glass multi-use towers. The city had squatted on the land for decades, waiting for developers to get desperate. Now the city had a sweetheart deal clutched in its greedy fist, and Ivan Coyote House faced demolition. Sure, the development proposal promised space in the new building for long-term care. Three hundred beds, as long as the developer didn't find a loophole and renege on the commitment. But where would Ivan's residents go? Dispersed to the suburbs to be forgotten, that's where. The city would never dedicate a shiny new home to old lesbians. No, when Ivan died, the city would never resurrect her.

Margaret squeezed her butt into the chair opposite the general manager's desk. It was an unforgivingly narrow seat, but she would have fit it with room to spare, once. Margaret checked the buttons of her cream silk blouse and smoothed her pencil skirt over her thighs. On the outside, she was perfect. A tiny bit fleshy, but plenty of former ballet dancers broadened out a bit. On the inside, well, it was obvious the manager could see right through to the fraud she was. The manager took his time settling himself in his big, black leather master-of-the-universe chair.

"I know what you're trying to do, Margaret," he said, finally. "And I can't believe you'd use your residents as pawns."

Margaret's breath left her in a puff, half-laughing from shock. "I don't have anything to do with this."

"You're trying to attract media attention."

"Attention for what? The residents came to visit the library. City Hall is our local branch."

"One of your staff is a stripper."

"Betty's a dancer—a burlesque artist. Let me see the security vid."

The manager slapped his laptop lid shut.

"The Ivan Coyote redevelopment is going forward. The final

vote happens on Friday. Lose the pink-haired girl and keep out of the media, or I'll have you shut down."

Margaret squeezed forward, perching on the edge of her too-small chair. "You can't shut Karen Kain down. We own the building—"

"If you try to block us," he interrupted. "The heritage department will review your building's appropriate-use status. Keeping a historic building in private hands is a waste. It's a city treasure."

Arguments whirled through Margaret's mind, but there was no point saying anything before consulting Karen Kain's lawyer. She bit her lip until the manager's power trip ran out of juice. She reassembled her dignity in the elevator and took her women home for lunch.

⋙ ? ⋘

Karen Kain's lawyer was an alarmingly hairy trans man with a gleaming smile behind an abundant raven-black beard. More hair poked out from between his shirt buttons and from under his cuffs. If David dropped his clothes in the middle of City Hall, Margaret thought, nothing would play peek-a-boo.

Nudity *per se* didn't bother Margaret. She'd spent years in crowded dressing rooms filled with sweaty dancers. Those were perfect bodies, though. Perfect like hers had been, once. Graceful, toned, hairless, elegant.

"Don't worry," David said. "Nothing can touch Karen Kain."

"It's not just the appropriate use review," Margaret said. "The residents have been acting up, and the manager said he could have us investigated for abuse. He could get our license yanked."

David laughed. "I'd like to see him try. We could hit the city with a dozen lawsuits. The billable hours would be massive."

Margaret stared at him. He laughed again and patted her hand.

"It's okay. Trust me. Karen's fine. Too bad about Ivan Coyote, though. I wish I could do something for her."

"Can't you?"

"There's no point. The city always planned to redevelop the lot. That's why they never properly maintained the building." He looked thoughtful. "And if you think about it, that's the only reason Ivan exists in the first place. Lesbians have little economic power and no political pull. They're easy to uproot."

Margaret nodded. She'd quit the ballet so she wouldn't have to face growing old in poverty. Many of the other dancers had husbands to bankroll their art. Margaret's few love affairs had been with other lesbian artists—a muscled sculptor who eked out a living as a community college sessional instructor, a spoken-word poet who cleaned offices on the graveyard shift, a photographer who worked in a day care. No savings, no pension; just one run of bad luck from homelessness.

Ivan was filled with women just like Margaret's old lovers, women who'd thumbed their noses at fate for decades in the name of rejecting patriarchy and not buying into the status quo. And now their last bulwark was about to fall. Ivan was just a charmless concrete slab, leaky, drafty, and remarkably energy-inefficient. Nobody would fight for her. But she was filled with women who would disappear if scattered. Who would fight for them?

Not Margaret. She'd made her choices, and she knew better than to fight a losing battle.

"You said no stripping on your clock," Betty said. "I'm on the clock, and I've got all my clothes on."

Betty's scrubs were patterned with 1960s pulp covers: teased bouffants and scarlet pouts above missile-shaped foundation garments. They disturbed Margaret, deeply. Not because of the inane titles (*She Wanted It; Babes Behind Bars; Trash Talking Tramps*) but because the models looked quite a bit like her mother.

Behind Betty, all the residents were crowded into the common room. Elsie, one of the oldest residents, posed in front of the fireplace, delicately shrugging the straps of a pink negligee off her age-spotted shoulder. The wattles of her upper arms quivered; her pursed mouth disappeared in a pucker of wrinkles. When Elsie's clothes finally dropped, pasties festooned with rhinestone pills dripped from the tips of her pendulous breasts.

One of the oldest residents was recording the show on her iPhone—probably live streaming direct to Facebook.

〜 ♪ 〜

Betty would have to go. She was a disturbance Margaret couldn't afford to tolerate. But when she called Betty into her office, Pia came too.

"Before you say anything, please let me speak." Pia looked over Margaret's head at Karen Kain, as if gathering courage. "I grew up in the Philippines, and I learned early on that women who love women have to be invisible."

Betty nodded. "Protective coloration."

"If I act just like everyone else," Pia added, "I can't be mistreated for who I am. But I'm not like everyone else. If I pretend to be what I'm not, who am I?"

"Pia," Margaret said. "This isn't appropriate. I need to talk to Betty in private."

"Betty's done nothing wrong. All she's done is be herself." Pia smoothed the front of her chrysanthemum-patterned scrubs. Then she reached out and took Betty's hand. "At some point, we must protect the people who are like us."

"Pia, it's not—"

"I know. It's not my responsibility to supervise the other staff members. But I've been here longer than anyone. If you fire Betty, I'll leave too. And I'll take all the staff with me."

After Pia and Betty had left the office, Margaret stared up at the poster of Karen Kain for a solid twenty minutes. *What Would Karen Kain Do?* Dance, of course. But dancing wouldn't help, not here, not now, not ever.

Words were the only weapon in Margaret's arsenal. She pulled out her favorite fountain pen and several sheets of creamy rag paper and began to write.

⁊ ⁊ ? ⁊⁊

Margaret fumed as she sat in the City Council visitor's gallery. The final hearing on the fate of Ivan Coyote House was the final item on a long agenda. The vote wouldn't happen until the early hours of Saturday morning. Of course, the city would schedule it at the end of a long session when everyone had gone home. Margaret would have to wait all night to make her speech. But would it even matter? She could speechify all she liked, but it wouldn't do any good if nobody was there to listen.

Margaret was wearing her best suit—the one she'd worn to her final interview with Karen Kain's board of directors. A tailored two-piece in gray wool: staid, responsible, and feminine. It said: "You can trust me with your multi-million dollar charitable foundation. I'm not going to do anything weird."

Protective coloration. Looking at Margaret now, who would guess what was really in her heart—how desperate she was, and how much she cared?

The general manager of Long-Term Care was sitting a few rows in front of her, the lights gleaming off a patch of shiny scalp barely concealed under a few strands of carefully combed, thinning hair. Margaret toyed with a metal tin of mints. The urge to toss them at him was nearly unbearable. She could hit his bald spot, easy, one by one. Embarrass him in public. He deserved it.

Margaret laughed to herself. *What Would Karen Kain Do?* Definitely not throw candy at a bureaucrat. High school tactics wouldn't get her far in life.

Opposite the visitor's section, the tiny media gallery emptied as the night wore on. At half past midnight, the council was still droning over a routine parks board report, and the last few journalists were packing up their laptops.

Ivan Coyote House was dead.

There was only one thing left to do.

Margaret shook the tin of mints. The loud rattle turned all the heads in the visitor's section. She shook them louder. Loud enough to be heard by the media gallery. The journalists paused for a moment, then went back to packing their laptop bags. She stood up and stepped gracefully onto the seat of her chair. The spike heels of her black leather pumps sunk into the padding, but Margaret was a dancer; she could perform on any stage.

The persistent rhythm of the mint tin raddle provided a compelling beat as Margaret flicked open the buttons of her high-necked blouse and slid the long sleeves down her arms. Her body wasn't perfect anymore, but it didn't matter. All eyes were on her, and there was no denying it:

The clothes were coming off.

SOMNOPHILIA

BY GEMMA FILES

*T*HE FANTASY'S DIFFERENT EVERY TIME SHE TELLS YOU ABOUT IT, spinning it out like some extra-fucked bedtime story. *I'm a nurse in a coma ward, and you're my favorite patient; I'm a die-at-home doula making sure your "end of life transition" goes like slipping into a warm bath. I'm a Victorian nanny, and you're my charge, almost old enough to move into your own room; there's a grown-up party, so I have to keep you quiet. I mix laudanum in your hot milk and watch you drowse in the dim gaslight, musing over what a man you've become until I just, I just ... can't help myself.*

Two fetishes for the price of one, and both of them creepy! you comment; she flushes. *That'd be why we're both adults, and they call it role-play,* she points out.

Or the Greek myth of Endymion: Selene, goddess of the Moon, beams down on a pretty shepherd, asleep with his flocks. She remembers her sister Eos, the dawn—how she fell for Tithonus and asked he be given eternal life, not realizing that without eternal youth he'd wither into a cricket, begging to die with every feeble chirp. So Selene asks Endymion to simply stay asleep, forever: young and handsome and unaware, drowsing the rest of his life away in sweet dreams of literally divine sexual gratification. Might've called it a bad bargain if he'd been awake, but he never got the chance.

Point is, all these fantasies have one thing in common: her awake versus you asleep, or close enough for jazz. Doesn't actually need you completely unconscious, just sedated, paralyzed, unable to consent or refuse, unable to fight back. To pose any sort of threat. *It's the only way I can do it, classic heterosexually,* she tells you. *Because of—things. That've happened, to me. You get what I'm saying?*

I think so, yes.

I mean—I like you, obviously, or we wouldn't be having this conversation. But I find men scary when sex is involved, even if they want me, or I want them; just need the upper hand when it's P in V, or it's not going to work. I need to be sure I can stop when I want, start when I want. Do what I want, with no ... interference.

And what is it you want to do, Lia?

She looks away, lips crimping. Says, finally: *I don't want to have to explain myself, either.*

All of which brings you here.

✖ ⁹ ✖

The good thing about Lia's fantasy is, unlike Endymion, you know you'll wake up, afterwards—that's the bargain, supposedly. The bad thing is how little you can remember about it, even now ... but that's what iPads were invented for.

The two of you lie full-length in the same bed that's currently front and center on your flatscreen, watching what feels like porn made by a comatose doppelgänger. Because that's you, naked, your breathing shallow and hitching enough to disturb; that's you, waxy-fleshed and slack, your eyes ticcing wildly under bruised lids. And that's Lia, also naked, swarming up over you from the bottom of the frame like some sexy nude reptile, her muscles coiling, predatory. That's Lia going straight for your slumbering crotch, mouth open wide as if she aims to swallow you whole, to chew your dick right off at the root—but it's also Lia in the here and now with her hand wrapped around your balls, kneading them gently in their sack like a bag full of marbles as she slips a leg up over your hip and humps herself against the meat-wrapped bone, so hot and wet already you can feel her slick your thigh on the way up.

No problems doing stuff when it's not P in V, I see, you comment, voice dry; she shrugs. *Not like this, no,* she says. *Not when you're ... watching us.*

Oh, uh huh.

Jane Toppan used to give her patients atropine and morphine, as a cocktail, she murmurs, in your ear, thumbnail flicking up your shaft's underside and back, a lizard's dry tongue. *Morphine to knock you out and keep you out, atropine to make your heart race, make you hyper-sensitive, make you think you're dreaming. Then she'd strip naked and get into bed with you, rub herself all over you, and masturbate to climax while you were dying.*

You feel your breath catch at the thought. *Is that what you gave me?* You can't help asking, but she just laughs, nipping at your lobe, hard enough to sting.

Of course not, she says, sweetly. *If I had, you'd be dead.*

Is that ... what you wanted to do?

And now you can feel her smile.

Just wait and find out, she says.

Onscreen, Lia is breathing then licking, licking then breathing, hot and wet, moist and cool; you can almost feel it, if only theoretically. You watch her catch the head of your dick in her mouth and pull, hard—watch the shaft start to fill, to blush, to darken. The head turns rosy, pumping out a bead of lube that Onscreen Lia tastes, delicately, before plunging herself back down and taking it as far as she can in one go, sucking hard. Her cheek and throat start to bulge.

Offscreen Lia chuckles and lets go of your bag, fingers ghosting up your crack, stroking at the tender outer edges, ringing your anus like she's tapping at a pursed-shut gate. *Turn over,* she tells you, but you shake your head. *Won't be able to see, then,* you reply, eyes still locked to last night, trying to remember what any of it felt like it—just the smallest quiver of sensation to match that image, in all its intensity, its immediacy: your empty face on top of a body in full bloom, in heat, flushing under Onscreen Lia's hands and body. Spreading itself wide at her urging, limbs out-flung, as she kneels up and kisses its cockhead with her clit, swipes it the length of her weeping slit—up, then down, then up again—before finally screwing herself down onto the whole thing, inch by inch. Her head thrown back and her chest heaving, nipples tight as beads, with a look on her face you can't easily interpret: could be ecstasy, or the opposite. Or ... maybe both.

Offscreen Lia is probably rolling her eyes, not that you can see. You can hear it in her voice, pointing out: *Can if you lean* forward, *you lazy bastard. Now—assume the position.*

Face down but eyes up, braced on your folded arms; Offscreen Lia slides a pillow under your hips, and you let her, you cooperate, hiking high. Not sure what's coming next, but you're game enough and quiet, at least 'til you feel her hands on your cheeks, her breath on your hole. Her breath, her kiss, her mouth, her lapping, probing tongue.

Oh, what—

Sssh. Keep watching. Don't look back, or I'll stop.

... well, don't do that.

Eyes riveted to the onscreen action, gasping as Offscreen Lia digs her whole face in between and starts excavating, juicily: sucks and nibbles, laps and licks, cracks you open a hair, then wider, then wider still. Wide enough for the tongue-tip, then the flexible, squirming muscle itself, penetrating you while you watch yourself penetrating her—that thing you can't remember ever doing, not even now, as you watch her strumming her own clit desperately with one hand while she slams herself up and down on *your* cock, hunching and gaping, twisting her own nipple painfully with the other. That same desperately hard cock now gravity-trapped beneath your flexing stomach's equally hard, hot flesh, sandwiched against the tucked sheets, grinding unconsciously back and forth as she stabs her tongue into you yet one more time, then yet one more, before at last replacing it with a pair of pussy-greased fingers. Feeling around inside you even as she rabbit-fucks them against your gut-walls, scissoring to get deeper; you can *hear* her riding her other hand as she pants, grunts, that wet slapping sound, that *churning*. And then—

Onscreen Lia screams, shaking all over, drooping, dropping forward. Onscreen you stay completely still, aside from a single heave of breath. Offscreen Lia hits that spot and hammers it as you hump yourself up on one hand, other grabbing, pumping, choking your own cock 'til it spits and keeps on spitting, 'til you both groan and mew and gargle your way to the end. 'Til you slump, and she clambers up, glues her chest to your back, crushing you in a way that'd be sweet if it wasn't so hot, so hard, so almost-hurting. If your ass and cock both didn't feel like they were bleeding.

Thank you, Lia says, muffled, into the skin between your shoulder-blades. And since you're too tired to tell her she's welcome, you just sigh into the mattress, closing your eyes.

Hey, Selene ...

Yes, Endymion?

That stuff you gave me. Any side effects?

Aside from the short-term amnesia? Nope.

A pause. Good thing we made a movie, then.

That's right.

Was any of that true, though? you ask as Lia lies beside you, later, snuggled together with your hands still tucked deep in each other's crotches, your spent cock asleep in her palm. Your fetish, your phobia ... not that I think you'd lie about something like that, I mean ... She's looking at you now, steadily, and you're surprised to find you can still blush, after everything that just happened. ... I'm sorry, you say, finally, embarrassed. Disappointed in yourself, especially if you never get to do that again.

Time ticks by—but then you feel her stroke her thumb across the head nail-first, quick as a bite, just to feel you shudder and leak. Look back up to see her eyebrows raise, mouth slightly quirked, as she shrugs.

And: Most things are at *least a little true,* she replies. Smiling.

Riding Yggdrasil

by Charles Payseur

RUNES DANCE INSIDE MY EYELID. EYE CLOSED, fist pumping, I see the incantations dance. They spell my name, hundreds of them—Fengr, Bragi, Gollorr, Runni vagna, Yggr, Odin—all one name, all spelling All-Father. They are magic, a litany of powers mine to command.

I want more.

More sensation, more magic, more knowledge, more feeling. I am Hangi now, the Hanged One, and my side aches and blood falls from the wound into the abyss. My breath hitches. I nearly lose myself.

"Niðhöggr incinerates the seed you spill into their pool," Ratatoskr cries, spoiling my rhythm. The pleasure ebbs. "And Mimir sips it along with the water from his. Will it grant him your favor? Your power? Your love?"

Damned squirrel.

I open my eye. The rodent sits above me on the branch around which my rope is secured. The fur on its ears forms horns that curl in the breeze.

"I will grant *you* a swift death if you do not leave now," I say through gritted teeth. My erection burns. After eight days, everything burns. I am reaching exhaustion, but there is something just beyond, something building inside me. Each new orgasm more intense than the last, every screaming pleasure more unbearable. The world blurs at the edges, the darkness an old friend knocking at the door, but I will not let it in.

Not yet.

"What secrets are you delving for, All-Father?" Ratatoskr asks. "Shall I tell the Eagle that you are pleasuring yourself so thoroughly to discern nir hidden name? Shall I tell Níðhöggr that you seek to feed the serpents that coil in wait below the world? Or maybe you know that Heimdallr is watching from his lonely post in Asgard, covered in his own ejaculate, sore and hungry but unable to look away? Does the thought of being watched arouse you, One Eye?"

"Peddle your scandals elsewhere, rat of the eagle's ass," I say. "Odin serves no other, and you will have no secrets from me."

The rest of the world, the rest of the Tree, is just a shadow now. What do I care about Heimdallr in his endless vigil? Or the worms that slither far below, gnawing at the roots of time? What do I care for the Eagle and its knowledge, or Níðhöggr and its hungry patience? My hand builds up momentum again. I hold a vision in my mind, of me on the tree, the noose around my neck. My whole body naked, streaked with blood and sweat and semen. My other hand squeezes my nipple, then the other, hard enough to pierce the aches and pains and encroaching darkness.

"Whatever your reasons, Spear Shaker," Ratatoskr says, "the whole of the Tree is watching, and most are hoping that you'll die here, your body food for ravens and worms."

I don't respond. Let them hope. Let them think what they will.

A noose is all that connects me to the world, my body bleeding, weak—let them think that I am trying to escape it all, the knowledge of the end of the world, the looming shadow of Ragnarök.

I imagine my body again, the bruising around my neck, the muscles straining. People misunderstand. They see only what they fear, death waiting for them at the hands of a brother, at the jaws of a wolf or a serpent. This has nothing to do with death, nothing to do with destruction or punishment. The darkness creeps in a bit further, and it's like I'm stepping outside of myself.

This is a celebration. If they see a sacrifice, then it is one of joy and abandon, myself for myself. I can feel my hand as my own and someone else's, and in my mind I am doubled, coiling around myself, alive. I open my second eye and something deep inside me stirs.

The touch on my chest is tender, trailing slowly higher. A wrinkled finger traces the curve of my lips, so dry. It opens my mouth, and I taste salt and the tang of semen. The hand on my cock is relentless, a stroke for each beating of my heart, ever faster, ever faster.

The finger leaves my mouth and moves serpentine down my body, barely avoiding the wound in my side, reaching around me and finding my ass. It is not gentle and the saliva does little to lube it as it forces its way inside. I moan like the universe collapsing.

I see everything now. The stars dance. Something is awake inside me, and my pleasure is building, building. Let them think I am running toward death, arms outstretched. I am not. But to deny it would be arrogant. Foolish. Even I, for all the power at my command, for all the magic coursing through me, tickling my prostate even now, even I will die. This rope, this tree—the entire universe is this tree—are just a bucking steer trying to throw me off. But I will not let go. I will ride.

I ride. The finger coaxes deep inside me and my throat is full of feathers, the world made of lights more distant than darkness. The wound in my side howls. There is a weight in my stomach like a stone, a hammer striking.

I come, and the pleasure of it burns away my second eye, burns away my second self.

I ride. There is something inside me, something dark and beautiful, and it tares free, guided by the finger still stroking my prostate. A shadow burst out of my cock, then another. The pleasure peaks. Far below the serpents hiss, and across the realms the air goes dry. Giants scratch their heads. The Norns frown. Heimdallr slumps to the ground, completely spent. The Eagle listens as Ratatoskr whispers into nir ear.

And two ravens, jet black and magnificent, streak through the air in front of my dangling form. My hands are my own again and fall to my side. The ravens circle, and take up their perches on my shoulders. Thought, they call, and Memory.

I smile, and reach, and grab hold of the rope. I pull myself up to the branch, remove the coarse braid from my neck. I am raw, and tired, and have a thirst that a river of mead would not cure. But I am alive. The future glitters before me like the interlocking scales of a serpent, like stars in the fur of a great wolf. The world is a tree, and the rope in my hands are the reins I will use to ride it to the very end.

KNITTED, KNOTTED, & BESOTTED

BY KAYSEE RENEE ROBICHAUD

*A*FTER TIRING OF THE RETREAD ARGUMENTS ABOUT why SCOTUS should not declare *Furry Fury* pornos volumes 1-16 criminal bestiality because they featured actual "ruff and ready" werewolves going at it, Dot changed topics to something personal, something real:

"My first exposure to stitches, at least when I learned how arousing they could be, was when I had to get the tip of my left ring finger sewn on after my cousin Darrel lopped it off with a shovel while we were playing archaeologists in Aunt Delores's flower bed. Nurse Liz in the ER, a woman with red and blue scrubs and shocking electric blue eye shadow, penetrated my skin with the needle and drew the black medical thread through, whispering to me how good I was being when I knew I was not good at all inside. Afterward, she gave me something sweet to suck on, a cherry Jolly

Rancher she had in her pocket. Later, when my disapproving daddy directed us to the family Ford station wagon chariot, I caught a view of Nurse Liz chatting and smiling with other nurses while smoking a cigarette.

"I dreamed about Nurse Liz's hands, the black thread. While awake, even though daddy told me not to, I peeked under the gauze and tape at the black threads holding me together. Later, I would sneak into the living room to watch mommy mending daddy's buttons. I especially enjoyed, breathless and unblinking as I gazed, while mommy penetrated the needle's eye with the colored strands. She had a white plastic box for her thread, shaped like wicker but it was just plastic. I snuck that into my bedroom for playtime. I told myself I was being good, even though I knew I wasn't. When mommy saw what I had done, boy did I get a talking to.

"I learned to stitch when I was twelve, and my finger had long since healed up just right. I stabbed myself as often, but that was part of the fun. A bloody thumb gets kissed. Soon enough, my stitches grew to be slight and neat and perfectly aligned. By that time, I was small and messy and terribly bent."

"And you got no straighter," Jannel said. She was sitting on the floor, cross-legged. Her fuck-me suit was a pleasing cream off-white leather contrasted beautifully with her redbone complexion. Corset cupping her breasts and squeezing her flanks, shorts with ties along the outside, garter belt, stockings with stitches instead of Cuban heels and seams. She called to the ceiling "Thank you God!"

"Shh," Dot said, pausing in her storytelling and adjustments she made to Marco's leather gimp hood. She wore lace accented with leather: tankini, boy-shorts, and ankle boots with spent bullet cartridges for stiletto heels. "Don't invite anyone else down here."

"If the Lord showed up," Marco said, "I would maybe have something to give him." The twenty-year-old Sicilian lay on the bed, two pillows bunched up behind his head and looking pleased with himself in his black leather chaps and no underwear, teasing the thick dark patch of hair on his chest because he had shaved his groin and balls until the fine, wrinkly skin remained naked and shivering in the breeze from the lazy spinning ceiling fan.

"Only if she tells you can," Dot said.

At this, Jannel raised her hand and turned it side-to-side, to both remind him she was present and still in charge of him.

"She likes when I misbehave," he said, making a kissy face.

"Because she likes to pound your ass until you bleed," Jannel replied with a disarming smile.

"Finished." Dot held up the gimp hood and inspected her work, turning it over in the corner floor lamp's pleasing glow.

Long laces drew up through eyes in the back, to snug it on the wearer's head. The eyes sealed behind a removable blindfold, the circle around the mouth was cinched with thick, surgical thread that could be pulled shut or released to allow airflow. The nosepiece had no breathplay options, so Jannel's glove placed atop would have to do.

Jannel examined the hood, playing with the threads on the mouth. "You do such fine, fine work."

Dot ran her eyes along the leather fuck-me suit and the body beneath. "I do, don't I?"

Jannel's demeanor changed in a heartbeat, going from amiable to boss bitch without hesitation. "Get the camera running, Dot." To Marco. "Time to get your ass over here, pretty boy. I want to tighten you up."

Dot moved the video camera atop the tripod. It was a small but expensive piece, the sort of digital component Marco claimed Troublemaker Studios on the other side of town used for second unit stuff. It was perfect for the amateur erotic entertainment they were shooting.

Dot gave a thumbs up that she was ready. Jannel, who was the director as well as the domme, said "Lights. Camera. Action."

Marco slipped into his sub role as smoothly as pulling on a jacket. Jannel caught him by the hair and dragged him to the floor.

"There." She pinched his nipples until even the ghost of his smile was gone. She spat into his open mouth. He was her whore, she assured him in a lover's whisper, and she was going to enjoy this.

Dot played the camera along both of their bodies during this exchange. Showing off the clothes and the deliciously sinful figures inside them.

Eventually, Jannel decided it was time for lights-out, making Marco's pretty features vanish under the supple material of Dot's hood. The mouth threading was wide, so he could gasp. Jannel tightened and tied the hood's rear laces, and each tug made the man's erection bob higher and harder. When she was done, he was panting and grinning and stiff as a beer bottle.

The questions and answers began, Jannel posing for the camera as she queried and degraded her sub:

Did he want her lips around that little erection? *Yes*, he replied, *please mistress.*

Did he think he was good enough for her mouth's ministrations? *Yes. He was good.*

No, she cooed, he was disgusting, and his cock was even worse. Too disgusting for her to touch without latex gloves. *Touch me*, he begged, *please touch me, mistress.*

He ate up this submissive role.

After tugging on a pair of leather gloves with rubber inset palms, she reached down to give him a squeeze and a jerk. It must have been too much because his whole body heaved with a spasm. However, he said, "Please don't stop!" But of course, she did because he needed to earn her attentions.

Dot closed in on Marco's mouth, the fullness of his lips and the powerful teeth behind them, the tongue that poked out to run across them.

Jannel asked about his tongue being good enough to taste her pussy. He pleaded, and they went back and forth until she decided he was too pathetic for that, which he happily agreed with. She allowed him to lick the sweat from her ass, instead. She slid down her shorts and mashed her ass against his face. Dot zoomed the camera to capture his gleeful tongue in motion. Jannel spared an off-screen wink and kiss for Dot. Marco really got into ass worship, savoring the sweat he lapped up and how his mistress ordered him to spear her asshole with his tasting organ.

Dot used the camera like surgeons used scalpels. Afterward, she would wield the editing software like sutures, pulling the whole mess together into art.

The seams appeared good on camera. The outfits glistened and emphasized the toned flesh sweating beneath. Jannel moved into money shot mode, cinching up her sub's mouth hole, so the stitches strained with his efforts for breath. She pressed her palm against his nostril slit while he finger banged her soaked, hot pussy.

The weakest stitches severed.

Dot called cut and rushed over.

Marco was panicking. "My hand! Where is my hand?"

"I have it, sweetcheeks," Jannel said. The appendage had come detached from Marco's wrist, and Jannel snatched it before deciding she wasn't done and used it like a dildo. After she came, a real one that made her sound a bit like a hyena instead of the porn star howling she did for the camera, she said, "There's a little present in your palm for later."

"Thank you, mistress."

Jannel unsnapped the blindfold, letting Marco see because

blindness and fear weren't conducive to play. She cradled his head to her belly while Dot worked.

He could not watch.

Dot inspected the damage and dragged out her white plastic box of needles and thread, a sewing kit just like mommy used oh, so many years ago. Dot used her care and precision to sew the hand back to the wrist, snagged a bottle of glowing green elixir from the fridge, penetrated the cap with a syringe needle and loaded it with a nice little shot. This needle entered his wrist between two of the small, neat, straight stitches.

The reanimation juice built flesh threads between severed tissues and imparted a lifelike color. Still, Dot said, "Let's take five and let that stuff work its science."

Jannel wiped Marco's tears and gave him a dose of Visine to battle red-eye. Today's scene was blindfolded but better safe than sorry.

He adored her when she fed his submissive kinks; he worshiped her at all other times. *Such a cute couple of dead kids.* Together, they made a perfect threesome.

Dot looked forward to joining them as reanimated kinks. Just a couple thousand bucks more and she could get the full surgery. Then, she would stitch them back together (as necessary) until the end of time. Oh, happy eternity!

DINNER WITH DANIEL
COLETTI

BY NATHAN PETTIGREW

*B*ETHANY KNEW I FANTASIZED ABOUT GETTING OFF IN PUBLIC PLACES—talkin' very public places with crowds and not just outside or under a bridge somewhere. Alone or with a partner, playing the scenario out in my mind was the only way for me to reach climax. Any chances to enact my fetish had yet to fall into my lap, but Bethany Coletti asked me to put my faith in her to make it happen.

I'd already placed my faith in her when agreeing to dinner with her parents, extreme right-wingers, at her father's strict request.

The host showed us to a booth in the bar area. When two Patriots fans clashed mugs, Corona and foam spilled out onto the orange tile floor. The heftier Patriot slouched with his hand on his buddy's denim ass. He moved in for the picture moment—the two men locking tongues—and Pastor Coletti stopped dead in holy shit.

He turned to the host. "Do you have any tables away from the bar?"

"Sure. Right this way." She brought us back through the smell of blue cheese and ground beef, and down to the establishment's opposite end where cinereous carpet divided small booths from longer ones against windows. "How's this?"

"That'll be fine," said Pastor Coletti. "Honey?"

Mrs. Coletti slid in first, struggling to fit between the seat's cushion and the table's edge.

I slid in across, scooting over and making room for Bethany.

Smiling, she held my stare while I pulled my arms free from my jacket. Her eyes were a thin brown over green, like caramel apples.

"Your waiter will be right with you," the host said.

"Okay," Pastor Coletti said. "Let's pray."

Pray? In public?

Bethany bowed her head. Mrs. Coletti did the same, setting her elbows on the table and leaning her forehead against folded hands.

Through thick glasses, Pastor Coletti kept his eyes closed while asking for God's will concerning the outcome of "tonight's talk."

Lord Jesus, come quickly. Amen.

He opened his eyes, finding my stare.

"So, Christopher, I understand you were baptized as a baby."

"I mean, I don't remember it, but—"

"Well, you were never truly baptized in the eyes of God," he said, "and if you're thinking about coming to church with Bethany—"

"Dad, we have to decide what we want."

When Pastor Colletti's attention fell to the laminated shine from his menu, Mrs. Coletti smiled.

"Sixteen dollars for a steak?" he said.

Her lips curled up to one side. "Sixteen's actually a good price, Daniel."

Bethany's soft, warm palm found mine under the table. She

massaged my knuckles, making this dangerous in the presence of her father who believed in "no physical contact" before marriage.

"So, Mrs. Coletti, Bethany says you have dachshunds."

This made her glow. "I have two."

Her husband glared at her. "Uh, honey? Let's stay focused. I was talking to Christopher about baptism."

The curves of brightness in her eyes caved into a cold, blank stare. "You're right, Daniel. I'm sorry."

She had too much gray hair for her age. Bethany had mentioned fifty.

"Christopher," Pastor Colletti said. "What are your intentions toward my daughter?"

I cleared my throat. "My intentions?"

The man's face stayed frozen, expressionless.

"Well, basically—" I cleared my throat again. "All I want, really, is for Bethany to be able to go places with me. You know, without hiding it from you."

"You're talking about courting my daughter," he said.

"Courting?"

"You call it dating, but dating is a worldly term I associate with immorality."

Bethany put more force into massaging my knuckles, pressing her thumbs into the valleys between.

"I'm cold," she said.

"Here. Take my jacket."

She spread the leather across our laps, bringing my hand beneath the jacket.

"Honey, would you hand me my Bible?"

Mrs. Coletti reached into her tote bag and pulled out a black Bible with Daniel Coletti written on the bottom corner of the cover in gold lettering.

"Nowhere in this book will you find anything about babies being baptized," he said, flipping pages. He slid the Bible m y way. "The book of Matthew. Turn to chapter twenty-eight, verse nineteen."

First glancing at Bethany for quick comfort, I flipped the pages and found the verse.

"As you can see," her father said, "that verse tells us to teach all nations, baptizing them in the name of the Father, and of the Son, and of the Holy Ghost. Do you think when talking about nations, it's referring to babies? How do you teach babies? Jesus was baptized as a grown man through immersion. He went down, under and came up again to foreshadow His death, burial, and resurrection. He openly accepted the will of His Father. Go to Matthew chapter three, verse sixteen."

Flipping pages, I fingered Bethany's palm beneath the table.

"That verse tells us that Jesus went up straightway out of the water," her father said. "Now he had to go under to come out in the way the Bible is teaching. Right?"

I placed Bethany's hand on my inner thigh, and she squeezed my crotch. I sat up. "I'd say so. Yes, sir."

With my forearm, I lifted the jacket a fraction, leaning closer to the table so no movement could be detected.

"Immersion is the biblical way," the pastor said.

I unzipped my pants.

"Immersion allows us to identify with the death, burial, and resurrection of Christ ...."

Bethany stuck her hand inside and pulled my dick out.

"We do it this way because we've been saved ..."

Twisting and pulling, her hand slid down and back up.

"We've accepted Christ as our Savior ..."

Down and back up.

"And through baptism, we're going public, so to speak."

Down and back up, going faster than before.

"Are you with me, Christopher?"

His daughter hung on to my hard display of blood, racing her hand against the rush.

"Yeah, I was just ..."

Down and back up, twisting and pulling.

" ... just thinking."

Bethany built me up to my fullest potential but not on my jacket—I moved the leather away to her lap.

And released.

Mrs. Coletti sat up, frowning.

"What's wrong?" her husband asked.

"My toes," she said, unable to see below her chest. "Something crawled on my toes. My leg, too, I think."

I grabbed a napkin. "I'll go under and look for you real quick."

"Oh, no, Christopher, there's no need for that," she said.

My head fell on Bethany's lap. Next, before anyone could say anything, I was down on my hands and knees.

The pastor let out a nervous, confused laugh. My nose came a breath away from his wife's skirt. She had two bloated stumps for shins, ghost white and glazed.

"It's just mayonnaise," I said, preventing awkward silence or worse.

"Mayonnaise?" she asked.

I brought the napkin to her flesh, careful not to let my fingers touch, and wiped, getting what I could while her husband started to slide out from the booth.

Shit.

I hurried, wiping her toes and the straps on her sandals, then came back to Bethany's stockings, and she helped me up from under the table. Her father stopped and eyed the crumpled napkin I shoved down into my pocket. Bethany couldn't look at him— because if she looked at him, she'd die from too much laughter— she wouldn't be able to stop.

"How in the world did I get mayonnaise on my leg?"

"Someone probably stepped on a condiment pack," I said. "You know, like how kids jump on a pack and it shoots across the room?"

She looked unsure, doubtful—a far sight better than devastated or all-knowing.

Her husband couldn't stop scanning the floor between their booth and those across the aisle.

"Dad? Were you finished talking?"

He shook his head, shaking off an absurdity he didn't have time to understand. "I think so. Christopher? Did you have any questions?"

I pressed my lips together. "None off the top of my head."

"Where do we stand on going out?" Bethany asked.

"As long as you're both clear on what we've discussed here tonight, I see no problems with you and Bethany going to that coffee shop you enjoy," he said. "Mrs. Coletti and I believe God put you in Bethany's life for a reason."

The blind fool couldn't see his daughter was the one deciding his level of involvement in our relationship. Out of respect—maturity—she didn't need his permission. She *allowed* him to give it.

The man may've given her life, but I helped her to be born again. Only one of us could make her a woman, and only one of us could hold on to her heart.

For Bethany, like her father's Savior, my mission was to endure long suffering. If that meant eating this man's holy shit for the foreseeable future, I would gladly oblige.

Bring all that you have to serve.

THE STONE BEAST

by Darien Cox

*G*ET THAT SLIMY DICK OFF THE TABLE! This is a pub. People eat here."

"It's not a dick." Remy's patience was wearing thin. "It's skin. It's just coiled up." He was reluctant to unroll the strip of skin he'd found in the forest. It had become precious to him, and he was wary this crew would want to touch it.

"It could be anything," the short bald guy at the end of the table chimed in. "It's probably from a snake or an alligator."

"It's neither," Remy said. "I'm a biologist. I tested it."

"It still looks like a dick."

Chuckles rippled through the small crowd around the table. Even the old historian guy in the sweater vest laughed.

Remy wasn't sure what he'd expected from a group he'd found on the internet. He was hoping for kindred spirits—people as obsessed with the Stone Beast as he was. But they'd scoffed at his proposal to hunt for it, despite the evidence he'd found. They didn't seem to want to do anything but *talk* about the damn thing

"Young man." Sweater Vest pointed. "I've written books on local folklore, and while an interesting myth, the *Stone Beast* doesn't actually exist."

"Then why do you even have this group if that's what you think?"

The old man shrugged. "To discuss using the legend to promote tourism. Bringing more money into the county helps everyone."

"It's real." Remy glared. "I've seen it."

The group roared with laughter. All but the young man sitting diagonally across from him. He was about Remy's age, blond, casual in a plain white tee shirt, arms crossed over his chest. Remy held his gaze, momentarily mesmerized by how attractive he was.

But the others were still laughing, which distracted him from the stranger's gaze.

"Fuck this." Remy stood, packed up his stuff and left the table.

"Oh come on!" the old guy called after him. "We want to hear about your sighting!"

More snickers followed as Remy exited the pub. It was a cloudy day, but he still squinted after sitting in the darkened room.

"Hey!" someone called out as Remy reached his vehicle.

Remy turned, surprised to see the cute blond guy approaching.

"It's Remy, right? I'm Paul."

"Hi. Uh ... can I help you with something?"

Paul smiled. "I can help you. If it's Stone Beast evidence you want, I can show you where to hit the jackpot."

"Are you screwing with me?"

"This your car? Let me in, and I'll take you there."

Remy hesitated. He wasn't one to invite strangers into his car.

"I've seen it too, okay?"

Eyeing him skeptically, Remy said, "Why should I believe you?"

Paul shrugged. "Stone Beast is supposed to resemble a statue, right? A beast made of gray stone. But it's not really gray. It's silver."

Stunned, Remy recalled the silver being he'd seen six months ago, darting out from behind a tree before sprinting off and disappearing from sight. He shivered, remembering the electric rush that had coursed through his body at the sight. "Okay. Get in."

After a short drive, Remy followed Paul down a muddy wooded path. He stopped before a massive split boulder edging a copse of trees. Paul turned sideways and slid through the rock opening, disappearing from sight. "In here," his voice called back.

Remy took a deep breath and followed.

The break in the entryway allowed some daylight into a small cavern. Beyond it, Remy spotted a gently flowing stream. The mineral scent of the water was strong. Paul picked something up from the ground. "Look."

Remy's eyes widened at the filmy thing hanging from Paul's fingers, like a snakeskin, but a foot wide, shimmering with silver. He let his eyes adjust to the dim light, then spotted more of them. The cave floor was littered with silver—thick peelings of it. Long, clawed footprints trailed across the mud heading to the stream.

Remy gasped. "This is fantastic. Shit, this could be a fucking lair or something!"

Paul dropped the skin and moved toward Remy. "Why are you so interested in the Stone Beast?"

Remy stumbled as Paul moved into his personal space. His back hit the damp wall. "I saw it."

"But why does it matter to you if the Stone Beast is real?" Paul stepped closer, their lips a breath apart. Unsure if Paul was going to kiss him or kill him, fear and arousal battled for dominance.

"Answer me," Paul whispered.

"Exploring the unknown gives me hope I guess," Remy said.

"Means there's more to this world than we know. That it's not so
..."

Paul pressed his body against him. "Lonely?"

Swallowing hard, Remy stiffened. "I was gonna say boring."

Nibbling along Remy's jaw, Paul whispered, "Are you bored
now?"

No, I'm confused and turned on. "What are you doing?"

Paul's fingers drifted up under Remy's shirt. "Exploring the
unknown."

Remy's insecurity told him a guy like Paul would never
be interested in a bookish nerd like him. But as trailing fingers
brushed over his nipples, Remy's swelling cock told his insecurity
to go fuck itself and run with it.

When Paul's tongue probed his lips and slid into his mouth,
Remy opened to him. Then there was nothing but deep, searing
kisses, the trickle of the stream and the sound of labored breath as
hands groped and shirts came off. When Paul's bare chest pressed
against Remy's, he was lost and knew he couldn't stop this even
if a Stone Beast itself walked up and tapped him on the shoulder.

"You taste good," Paul breathed against his lips.

Remy's hips lurched, aching for contact, hissing when the
bulge in Paul's jeans brushed his own. But as much as he wanted
more, more skin, more touch, more everything, Remy was caught
off guard when Paul stepped back and kicked off his shoes, then
stripped out of his jeans, leaving him naked.

Shivering as his gaze trailed over Paul's smooth muscled body,
Remy whispered, "We can't do this here." His eyes dropped to the
long, full cock pointing at him, then up to Paul's smiling face. "Can
we?"

Paul fell upon him, devouring his mouth while his fingers
tugged Remy's jeans open. "We can," he huffed as he freed Remy's
straining cock, shoving his jeans over his hips and taking his briefs

with them. "If you want to. Do you want to?" Paul squeezed Remy's cock and stroked.

Remy's shoulders hit the cool stone wall as his back arched. "Yes," he said without further hesitation. "Oh fuck, yes."

Paul kissed him, stroking Remy's cock, twisting each time he reached the head, making him see stars. With his jeans still around his ankles, Remy's thighs were pressed tightly together, and he hissed when Paul's cock slid between them. Each thrust of Paul's cock between his thighs tickled Remy's balls, the myriad of sensations pushing him toward the edge. Paul's cock glided easily between his legs, surprisingly slick already, and Remy's arousal skyrocketed at the evidence that this hot guy was as turned on as he was. *Turned on by me.*

"Fuck!" Remy broke the kiss as Paul stroked him faster, pumping between his thighs. "I'm gonna come."

"Me too."

Remy felt the warm release of Paul's climax coat his legs as his own cock gushed over that pumping fist. He stared into the other man's eyes as bliss pulsed through him.

His eyes. Oh fuck, his eyes.

Pushing Paul away, Remy tugged his jeans up and stumbled, gasping as he moved toward the entrance. He blinked and squinted, concluding that it wasn't a trick of the light making Paul's skin silver, and his pretty blue eyes now yellow with a vertical black slit.

Shock threatened, but the neurochemical bliss of climax still thrummed, so as revulsion tried to break through it was buffered by afterglow. For those few seconds of confusion, Remy didn't mind the silver skin, the strange yellow eyes, or even the sticky evidence of release dripping down his legs. He nearly took a step toward the beast.

Paul reached for him with a clawed shimmering hand. "You were amazing," he rasped, voice thick and gravelly.

Claws. Those clawed hands had just been on his dick. That revelation jolted Remy out of his hazy spell, terror finally muscling through and taking over.

Remy turned and fled, slipping through the rock opening. He didn't stop running until he reached his car. With trembling hands, he got the key in the ignition, floored the gas pedal and tore off down the road.

Through the entrance of the cave, Paul watched Remy go. A splash disturbed the stream behind him, making him turn, as his brother walked toward him, silver skin dripping with water. "You brought one of them *here?*"

Paul smiled, replying in his own language, "It was worth it."

"You have to stop doing this. You're risking exposure, and they could have diseases!"

Shrugging, Paul turned and stared out at the woods, satisfied from the sex but disappointed it was over. "I can't help myself. Fucking them is a passion."

"It's a fetish. And it's disgusting. Don't do it again."

He heard his brother retreat, then slip back into the water. "I won't do it again," Paul said softly as he gazed out at the woods.

But he knew he would. As soon as possible.

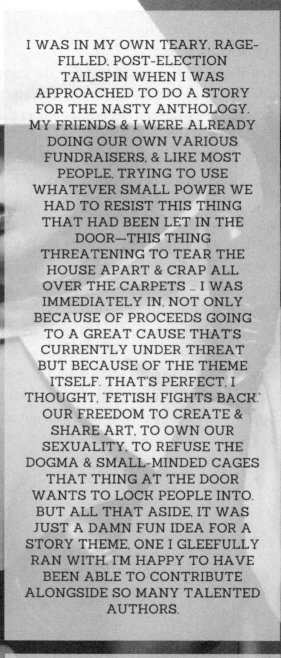

I WAS IN MY OWN TEARY, RAGE-FILLED, POST-ELECTION TAILSPIN WHEN I WAS APPROACHED TO DO A STORY FOR THE NASTY ANTHOLOGY. MY FRIENDS & I WERE ALREADY DOING OUR OWN VARIOUS FUNDRAISERS, & LIKE MOST PEOPLE, TRYING TO USE WHATEVER SMALL POWER WE HAD TO RESIST THIS THING THAT HAD BEEN LET IN THE DOOR—THIS THING THREATENING TO TEAR THE HOUSE APART & CRAP ALL OVER THE CARPETS … I WAS IMMEDIATELY IN, NOT ONLY BECAUSE OF PROCEEDS GOING TO A GREAT CAUSE THAT'S CURRENTLY UNDER THREAT BUT BECAUSE OF THE THEME ITSELF. THAT'S PERFECT, I THOUGHT, 'FETISH FIGHTS BACK.' OUR FREEDOM TO CREATE & SHARE ART, TO OWN OUR SEXUALITY, TO REFUSE THE DOGMA & SMALL-MINDED CAGES THAT THING AT THE DOOR WANTS TO LOCK PEOPLE INTO. BUT ALL THAT ASIDE, IT WAS JUST A DAMN FUN IDEA FOR A STORY THEME, ONE I GLEEFULLY RAN WITH. I'M HAPPY TO HAVE BEEN ABLE TO CONTRIBUTE ALONGSIDE SO MANY TALENTED AUTHORS.

DARIEN COX

METAL

BY LAZULI JONES

*S*O, UM ... IS THIS GOING TO HURT, OR ... ?"
Stella squirmed on the reclined leather-padded
chair.

"Well, yeah, *habibti*. But that's kind of the point, isn't it?" Jihane
knelt, running her hands over Stella's clothed breasts, finding the
nipples through the fabric, and rolling them in her fingers.

Jihane's thick black hair was pulled up into a casual bun, and
as her hands worked, she smiled and flicked the tip of her tongue
against the snakebite piercings on her lips—tiny, green jewels
against thick, dark lips.

Stella gulped and lifted her hips to let Jihane pull down her
jeans and panties.

"Mm ..." Jihane said. "But think of how gorgeous that pussy's
going to look once it's all decorated." She stood and checked her
equipment. Jihane had on a short, black skirt. Aside from the
meticulous tattoos covering calf to thigh, her copper legs were

117

bare. Farther up those thighs and under that skirt was nothing but bare pussy and a shining topaz jewel adorning her clit."

Stella loved the sight of that topaz. Her pussy pulsed, and as the cool air teased her, she was getting wet. It didn't take much more than a few clever twists of the topaz to make Jihane scream though a shattering orgasm. Stella had been fascinated, curious about the intensity. An idea leading up to tonight's illicit tryst had been seeded.

"It's a good pain. Trust me," Jihane said. She turned around with a tray of instruments in her hand: clamps, needles, antiseptic wipes, latex gloves. On a separate tray, she placed a small titanium barbell.

Many customers had been tattooed and pierced in Jihane's parlor, but only Stella would receive the *real* special treatment.

When Jihane was satisfied everything was ready, she smiled and lifted the hem of her tank top. Two large-gauge rings adorned each dark swollen nipple—Stella often managed to make Jihane come just by tugging on those nipple rings.

"Come here," Stella said.

Jihane ran her fingertips against the nipple rings before straddling Stella's thighs.

Stella put her hand against the Persian writing tattooed on the back of Jihane's neck, pulling her in for a kiss. While her tongue explored Jihane's mouth, her hand wandered below Jihane's skirt, rubbing along smooth skin, finding moist curls and soaked folds. Stella worked her finger around until she found the object she and her girlfriend loved so much—the vertical barbell set with a topaz running through Jihane's clit. Two quick little flicks of the barbell and Jihane quivered, moaning, against Stella.

Jihane was tall, tattooed and glinting with metal all over her body: four piercings in each ear, a ring through her eyebrow, one in her nose, snakebites in her lips, a stud through her tongue, thick rings through both nipples, and of course, the topaz on her clit.

Stella had no ink and hardly any metal, but she loved Jihane's piercings like a dying woman loved water. Stella loved playing with Jihane's metal, twisting them through the copper skin, listening to her girlfriend describe the sensation.

Jihane's fingers found Stella's pussy, freshly shaved, and Stella squirmed in the chair, spreading her legs as Jihane's fingertips ran along the smooth outer skin, teasing the silky wetness that led up to her clit. In response, Stella captured the topaz between two fingers, brought Jihane down on her for another kiss, and moved her fingers back and forth.

Jihane's tongue stud slid against the roof of Stella's mouth, tickling her, sending her warm and pleasant memories of that stud working all over her pussy. A few more twists of the barbell between her fingertips and Jihane started as though shocked, grinding down hard on Stella's thigh, and as she came, leaving behind silky wetness.

As Jihane found her footing, she had the easy, lazy smile of someone fresh from orgasm, her hand still teasing Stella's pussy with a touch meant to arouse but not to make her finish—that would come soon enough. Stella smiled at the sight of her beautiful girlfriend flushed and out of breath, and she cupped both of Jihane's breasts before tugging on the nipple rings.

"You're distracting me, *habibti*. You're not nervous, are you?"

"Nervous? Just because my girlfriend is about to stick a needle in my business?"

"Just think of how good it'll feel," Jihane kissed Stella's mouth, rubbing her snakebites against Stella's bottom lip, and began working her way down Stella's body. A lick with the tongue stud was chased by a kiss. Around Stella's breasts, the stud worked and swirled around each nipple before Jihane's mouth closed around each one in turn.

Stella gasped and spread her legs wider. How would it feel to have the needle driven through her nipples? The thought made her even wetter.

Jihane worked her way lower, pressing a final kiss to Stella's shaved mound before pulling away. Stella's head fell back against the leather seat—she tried to ignore the clink of instruments on the tray, the snap of latex gloves. Jihane gently spread her folds, but instead of a tongue, the coolness of an antiseptic wipe greeted her pussy.

"Shit, that feels weird," Stella said.

"Do you want me to warn you before I do it?"

"No."

Stella bit her lip, her legs trembling as she struggled against the impulse to close them. Sweat gathered on her brow and collarbone, and as cold metal clamps closed around her flesh, she shut her eyes, thin king of the little topaz in rich black curls. Jihane's fingers worked in silence.

Anticipation bubbled in Stella's stomach. A touch on her lips was gentle, soothing.

"Breathe in ..." Jihane whispered. Her wrist brushed the inside of Stella's thigh, making her shiver.

Stella stared at the ceiling, drawing in a long, wavering breath, listening to the soft clinks from whatever her girlfriend was doing down there. Every brush of Jihane's arm against her skin made her tingle, left her teetering on the brink of ... something.

"Breathe out ..."

Stella did, breathing out with a strangled exhalation. By the time the breath left her body, it was replaced by a sharp, all-consuming shock of pain.

Pleasure chased pain, or maybe it was the other way around.

She stung and burned and pulsed in waves—coming like she'd never come before—her body quaking until the pleasure-pain of her orgasm was replaced by a soothing rush of endorphins.

Metal clanked against metal. Jihane cooed soothingly. Nimble fingers worked at her sore yet excited flesh, and with a final wipe of antiseptic, Jihane stood from between Stella's legs, and careful to keep her distance from the fresh-pierced area, straddled her thigh.

Jihane kissed her, rubbing her rings against Stella's lips. "Relax. Savor it. You took it like a champ. And now, you look like a fucking queen. I'll put in something shiny and blue when you're healed—it'll look amazing."

"Holy shit," Stella said. The leather was hot and sticky against her skin, her clit throbbing like mad. "Did you come like that when you had yours pierced?"

"I almost kicked the guy in the nose. And if you think that's good, wait until it heals. Meaning, unfortunately, we'll need to abstain for a little while until it does."

Stella nodded, a little disappointed, but if it meant more of this, she could wait a few weeks. She kissed Jihane, running her thumbs over the bumpy rings in the dusky nipples, and planned her next metal.

Maps for a Worm

by Jason S. Ridler

BIRTHED IN A SHY HEART, OBSERVING THE world around you from the worm's eye view. Not wide eyes, not bold, but sly. Eyes down to see the stomp, trample and rush of feet marching as if to war.

A cadence you wish to follow.

One glance and everything tightens, the suffocating joy braced by shame. But we know who you are. What you are. Let us prove we've done our homework. Sit and be good.

As if you had a choice.

Mother's first.

Always in hose, her white skin turned tan, as if to smooth out all rough edges . . . Something snaked beneath the surface.

There's no shame now. You called us, remember? Closing your eyes? We know it won't help. And so do you.

The bumps emerging from secret skin, as if they were fingers in gloves, the trace of dark lines across the top of her feet a signature in faded green. The contours of imperfection excited you.

Then mother's flats walked away, signature lost.

Hush . . . She was only the beginning. How quickly desire constricts.

Leaving was the best thing she could do. Then you could steal the world with your eyes. School was a boon. Not the girls in class. They were loud, annoying, hurtful. But the teachers. Pumps and Sabrinas and hose, stocking and tights covered a cavalcade of joy. Especially your principal.

Oh, look, friction . . . We love how nostalgia grips you. Early imprints are so precious.

From toes to nose, she was eye candy, but like a peep show, you started at the bottom, crawling your way up . . .

Mmm. Yes. A worm that peeps is a low worm indeed. You are no alpha mutt, grabbing ass and breast. You worship with your eyes.

Serve us head down. We know. We love it. All of it.

She was powerful. Two-inch heels at all times. Sharp. She clacked down the hallway, so you knew she was coming. Pumps, never flats. Black and shiny. Purple and summery. Nude and dreamy.

And always with hose, black, brown, nude, that covered up a network of green webs etched like tattoos of maps to foreign kingdoms. From the top of her foot, crawling up her calves, both sides, under the whiter flesh of her knee. From beneath the mask of pulled fabric and leading up her skirt into parts unknown, a journey your mind took every night as your body dreamed of her clicking across the kitchen floor, raising a purple pump and kicking you onto your back . . .

Breathless, she stands above you in a purple skirt and blazer, nails and lips bright. Her face, a matron who thought she was a queen, crows feet thick with makeup, blush and eye shadow hiding her growing years, a hard, old beauty with straw-blond hair and a crooked nose that made you ache. Heels stabbed your ribs as you reached up and felt the smooth burn of stockings and underneath, a thick vein like an e xtension cord, pulsed with life. Pulsed with you. Heartbeats kicking in synch.

And her words, only for your ears. "Find me. All of me."

And your hand gripped her flesh and made her gasp then it slid up the vein's trail, higher, and higher—

Too much. Don't move. We're not even close to done and neither are you.

You hated winter when she wore boots, only her knees exposed between the cuff of her boot and the hem of her skirt, that knee encased in sheer black stocking pulled so tight you could glimpse it . . . The map, the one that started in the web beneath her toes, the one that climbed up her thigh, past her skirt, into darkness.

And you knew the path you wanted, that made you ashamed.

You collected maps of veins. Like other men collect youthful conquests, your notches were different. You studied the maps of managers of designer dress shops, places where heels and stockings made their veins flex. You never took a job in retail unless your boss was a woman, and only stayed if she had her map on display. For years, that was enough.

But not today.

Which is why you called us.

Which is why we're here.

Ah, see? See how strong you are when you admit what you are? Now, let's make things tight.

Look at us. Each heel. Each crinkled ankle. Each painted nail pushing our stockings thin.

We did our homework. Not one of us is weak. Not one of us is in flats. Not one of us is a girl.

Because we know you need women. Lots of them. And there's no shame in that. Especially with maps this thick. Can you see them beneath the silk? Don't you want to touch them . . . Lick them through the sheerness, ride our legs up into the darkness . . . Don't you want to hear the sound we make when your tongue is burning a path upon our thigh, your head swimming with darkness as you follow the map to its final destination, suckling at our breasts as we wrap our veins around you?

Do it.

Ahh . . . Taste it. Follow the flavor of our wrappings.

Taste them. Follow our map. *Taste it,* tear it, until crimson bliss stains your mouth.

Good boy.

ACTS OF CONTRITION

BY SELENA KITT

I WAS IN BOARDING SCHOOL, AND THINGS WERE different back then. I think they still have corporal punishment in some states, like Texas, but in most places it's been phased out. But we were good Catholics, or we were supposed to be, and if you spared the rod, you'd spoil the child. Hell, that was what my parents put me there for in the first place. My father couldn't stand to say no, and my mother couldn't say anything but, and they de cided, between them, that someone else should raise their daughter.

So the nuns and the priests attempted to curb my voracious appetites for four years. They failed miserably. By the time I was a senior, my birthday just passed in a haze of alcohol and sex—the drinking age hadn't yet been changed from eighteen—I'd been disciplined more times than I could count, suspended from classes, and nearly expelled, twice. I was always scraping by, just barely, but it was enough for me.

Father Hamilton had the task of disciplining me for my latest transgressions. The nuns had pretty much given up and handed me over to the priests, which was fine, as far as I was concerned. The priests were more direct. They liked to use the paddle—a thick piece of wood that Father Lowery, who taught physics, had drilled several holes through for less air resistance—and while it stung, it was over pretty quick. And the good thing about Father Hamilton was that he hated to give sermons. It was always straight to the punishment.

"Over the desk, Amy."

I knew the drill. I bent over his wide desk and lifted my skirt—they weren't supposed to touch us except with objects—exposing the seat of my white cotton panties. It was a typical school uniform, navy skirt, white blouse, white knee socks, Mary Janes. We looked like drones running up and down the halls on our way to class.

"For every blow, you must say an act of contrition."

"Yes, Father."

I waited, my heart hammering in my chest. I wasn't afraid of it anymore, but there was a sick sort of anticipated dread anyway in the moments before.

SMACK!

I winced, beginning:

"Oh my God,

I am heartily sorry for having offended Thee,

and I detest all my sins

because I fear the loss of heaven

and the pains of hell—"

The second SMACK! came long before I could finish, and I began again with a gasp, "Oh my God, I am heartily sorry for ..."

SMACK!

SMACK!

SMACK!

"Father!" I whimpered, my whole ass on fire with pain. It hadn't been like this before. "Please!"

"That's right," he murmured. "Beg."

SMACK!

"Oh!" I buried my face in my arms, trying to hide from the pain. "Oh please, I'm sorry, please ..."

"You've been in my office fourteen times this year, Amy." SMACK!

"And you've said an act of contrition for each blow." SMACK! "And yet you're still running around like the whore of Babylon aren't you?"

I would have screamed when he grabbed my hair, pulling my head back as he growled this last, but my voice was gone. I thought Father had gone crazy.

"What will it take to get through to you, girl?" He shook my head, back and forth, and I looked at him with wild eyes. His whole body pressed me against the desk, the weight of him incredible, and I gasped for breath. "This thing is useless with you!"

He threw the paddle and it clattered on the marble floor. "Your sins are of the flesh. Perhaps you need a lesson in that."

He let me go and I collapsed on the desk, feeling tears stinging my eyes, rolling down my cheeks, although I fought them.

"Perhaps ..." His voice had turned thoughtful, and I chanced a puzzled glance back over my shoulder just in time to see his hand coming down toward my ass.

SMACK! The solid sound of flesh on flesh filled the room, and he did it again. SMACK! SMACK! SMACK! I cried out, trying to wiggle away, but he grabbed my hips, pulling my panties down to my knees, and kept going, a steady rhythm, over and over. SMACK! SMACK! SMACK!

"Please Father!" I sobbed. I'd forgotten all about hiding my pain, my fear—and I was afraid now. He was crazed, mad, and I didn't have any idea what he might do. "Please, I'm sorry! I've sinned, I've sinned, I'm sorry... sorry for having ... offended ... Thee ... owwwww!"

His hands spread my legs wide, pressing my thighs open and my eyes widened in panic and a dawning horror. "Sins of the flesh," he muttered, and I felt his body pressing, his robes lifting, parted, and the heat of his crotch against the stinging, reddened globes of my ass.

"Father, please!" He grabbed my hair again, and I sobbed when he shoved his cock into me, the final humiliation.

"You need a good lesson," he grunted, thrusting deep. I whimpered, unable to believe this was happening, that a priest had just impaled me across his desk and was now beginning to fuck me. I'd been fucked before—I loved it—but this? This was a horror, an abomination, a ...

"A good ... hard ... lesson!" Each word was punctuated by a thrust, and his hands found his way underneath me to grab my breasts through my blouse, shoving it aside and tearing off a button to reach under my bra and squeeze my flesh.

"The paddle doesn't work." He gasped when he felt my nipples hardening. "Maybe you need a lesson from the holy staff!"

"Oh God," I moaned as he pounded me harder, his fingers squeezing both of my nipples, sending hot shocks down to my pussy. I was wet—God help me, I was wet, and his cock was pumping fast, his thighs spreading mine wide, driving me toward the deepest sin I'd ever known.

He'd gone crazy, and I was going crazy right along with him. My cunt was on fire, my nipples burned, and I knew we were both going to hell, but I didn't care. Father Hamilton groaned when I squeezed my pussy around his cock, arching, fucking him back.

"You're a bad girl!" He smacked my ass, hard, and I jumped, the sensation vibrating through me. "Bad!" SMACK! "Bad!" SMACK!

"Fuck!" I cried, spreading wider, wanting more. "Yes!"

"Ahhhhhhhh, God, forgive us all!" He groaned, grinding his hips into mine, and I trembled beneath, feeling my climax coming and unable to stop it. I was beaten, broken, humiliated, and completely at his mercy as I writhed in my own pleasure on the desk while he fucked me senseless. I didn't have time to think or breathe or speak when he grabbed me again by the hair and shoved me down to my knees on the floor.

"You will be penitent!" He insisted, shoving his cock deep into my throat with a low groan. I gagged, but I took it, hearing him whisper, "I am your bread and wine," just before throwing his head back and letting go. My mouth flooded with cum and I choked, swallowing, tears streaming down my face as I took it all, every last bit, looking up wide-eyes at this priest, this man I didn't know anymore, wearing black robes and a white collar.

He moved away from me then, leaving me gasping on my dirty knees, mascara streaked down my cheeks, blouse torn open, pussy dripping. His robes fell back into place and he leaned against the desk, breathing hard, composing himself.

Finally, he waved his hand toward the door, not looking at me, "Go."

I stood on shaky legs, wobbling toward the door, when I heard him say, "You will return tomorrow for further punishment. We aren't done yet."

No. No we weren't done, I discovered. Not by a long shot. Father Hamilton's punishment went on and on, until I thought I would die from the pleasure and the pain, a nd my only fear was that it might end. But it didn't. Thank you, God, it didn't.

He continued to punish me, not sparing the rod, every single day for the rest of the year.

PRICK AND PERSUASION

BY MOLLY TANZER

*S*HE MARKS HER PLACE WITH THE RIBBON before shutting the hardback copy of *Dubliners.*

"Well?" he asks, powering down his Kindle and turning over in bed to face her, head propped on his hand. "What did you think?"

He's eager for her to have enjoyed it, and is confident she did; she can tell from the way his dark eyes shine at her. She fights the urge to run her fingers through his chest hair, just like she likes.

That can wait.

"I liked it," she says, being completely honest. "It was good."

"'Good!'"

She nods. "When his uncle doesn't come home, and he's so frustrated ... I remember feeling like that, as a child. As if adults were awful, obscure, unfair—as if I would never get the chance to live my life."

"Yeah," he agrees. "I'm surprised you never read it before, even just "Araby"—it's been anthologized so often."

Just to tweak his nose a bit, she waves her hand in a vague motion and says, "Well, you know. Short fiction just isn't all that relevant anymore."

He takes the bait. "*Dubliners* was published in 1914."

"It's 2017."

"I'm aware. And yet, Joyce remains the greatest writer in the English language."

She laughs at this outright. "No way!"

"Yes, way."

"No, no way! Even if you could make that case for his short fiction, you certainly can't for his novels."

"Who's better?"

Without a moment's hesitation, she says, "Jane Austen."

He sits up in bed as if she'd nominated someone completely outrageous, like Dan Brown, or Ayn Rand.

"Nothing Jane Austen wrote can compare to *Ulysses*," he says with total certainty.

Teasing him turns her on; she's been hoping he'd respond to her dig about the state of short fiction by initiating a bit of rough sex, just like she likes, but the dig at Austen brings her focus entirely to their conversation. "How is that?"

"Well, for starters, *Ulysses* employs the structural play of a modern novel while still evoking the classic 19th-century tale of a young man gadding about a city. It's trying to do more with the novel form."

"*The novel form,* as you say, had barely been around for a hundred years when Austen was writing, and Joyce has another hundred on her! No fair judging medieval painters for not employing chiaroscuro."

"Maybe, but Joyce broke English wide open and then put it back together again, all while hearkening back to the Classical past. Instead of the winedark sea, he gives us the scrotumtightening sea."

"Oh, pfft. Jane Austen was just as clever at being dirty, and more elegant about it—like in the scene in *Pride and Prejudice* where Darcy tells Miss Bingley he'd rather jerk off alone than fuck her."

"I don't remember Colin Firth saying that in the miniseries."

"Well, not in so many words, but it's in there! The letter-writing scene. When Miss Bingley suggests mending Darcy's pen, that's her offering herself up; Darcy replies that he always mends his own, which is a pretty clear indication of his preferences. So, you can keep your tight scrotum." She leers at him. "And your fart-sniffing."

The sigh he utters could only be described as long-suffering. "Why do people always bring up fart-sniffing whenever someone expresses an honest enjoyment of Joyce?"

"I can't speak for others, but for my part, it's because until you made me read "Araby" the only Joyce I'd read was a listicle of his best dirty lines."

"Made you read it, did I?" He paws at her, pushing her onto her back. Delighted to have successfully provoked him, *finally,* she grins up at him as he sheds his boxers and climbs atop her chest, pinning her arms with his knees. It hurts a little, just like she likes."You've got quite a nerve, do you know that? I strongly recommend you give yourself a gift by reading one of the most poignant stories ever written, and you thank me by talking about fart-sniffing."

"He was pleased his lover had an arse 'full' of farts if memory serves; Joyce described them with gusto."

He starts pulling obscenely at his cock. "Yes, I've read his letters—all of them, you know, not just a *listicle.*"

"Is it the feeling of intellectual superiority that's getting you so hard, or the discussion of—mmf."

He's covered her mouth with his unengaged palm. "You've inspired me, my dirty little fuckbird. Since you like letters so much, and pens, I'll think I'll write you a one with *my* pen—all over your face."

She makes a muffled sound and he takes back his hand. "Scoot forward a bit, and I'll tighten your scrotum while you think about exactly what it is you wish to say." She waggles her tongue at him lasciviously. "I might not be the sea, but I think I can get the job done."

He does so. The relief in her arms is immediate; she stretches them, waggling her fingers to get the blood back into them before gently probing his asshole as he lowers his balls into the moist cavern of her eager mouth.

"That'll keep you from talking any more about farts," he grunts, spreading his legs wider so he can press himself down harder. With her lips stretched wide, her nose buried in his crotch, eventually, she is forced to tap his bottom to beg for a breath of air. He sits up a bit; she inhales, he fills her again. Uttering a muffled groan, she swirls her tongue over his loose skin; his hand's pace quickens over his shaft and he backs away. His balls escape her lips with an audible pop.

"Are you going to come?" she asks eagerly, gazing up at him as he yanks at himself yet more frantically.

"Yes I said yes!" he cries at the crisis, getting it in her hair, but missing her eye.

He wipes up the worst of it with a handful of tissue, then cuddles her to his chest. She listens to his heart pounding, pleased to have pleased him.

"I wonder if Lizzie ever did that with Mr. Darcy," she muses softly.

"What, you don't have some ready passage at hand to point at and claim Austen was clearly saying he gave her a face full of come every night?"

"Better a face full of come than an arse full of—"

"Shh," he says.

HUMILIATION

BY LUCIEN SOULBAN

OOK AT YOUR HERO!"
Stalwart struggled, but he felt like a ten-ton nail hammered into the AstroTurf by a hundred-ton sledgehammer.

"Instead of being graced with God, you got the statue of one, instead," Primacy said, cackling.

The ground cratered around Stalwart the harder he fought against the forces imprisoning him. The sand beneath the artificial grass was giving way, the draining stones beneath cracking and breaking. The tide of the device was overwhelming, and not with any fundamental force of nature. His muscles had been highjacked and turned against him. He buckled to his hands and knees.

"You want someone to worship?" Primacy bellowed. "Worship me!"

One moment, Stalwart was basking in the adulation of the stadium, their cheers thundering against his titanium-infused chest, the next moment they were all hostages to the supervillain,

Primacy. Nobody moved, everyone locked in place, staring at Stalwart in his blue and white costume, pleading for their hero to explode free and snap Primacy's thin neck. Well, not that he would kill the purple-costumed villain. He'd lose so many endorsements. A hero needed a villain after all.

"Aren't you going to save these people?" Primacy demanded as he fiddled with the chrome rod that was keeping the crowd prisoner.

Stalwart had played this game before with countless other villains, being captured, the gloating that followed, and Stalwart always freed himself at the appropriately dramatic moment because, let's face it, he could have escaped at any time. Frankly, letting himself get captured and suffering through insufferable monologs was part of the job. When depleted uranium bullets and plasma weapons barely gave him a thrill, he needed something to nudge the old heart rate past 70 BPM.

The thrill only came when he was tied down and could almost imagine himself helpless and exposed, imagine the villain reaching down and squeezing his ... bread and eggs. That's when something stirred between his legs. But the fantasy never lasted. He was never truly helpless and the villains were only interested in themselves.

Until now.

For the first time in ages, Stalwart couldn't struggle hard enough, and it left him kneeling with his head bowed, sweat dripping from his palms. With that, came the sweetest surrender. He could finally let go.

Someone else had the control.

The stirring returned, stronger than ever and rooted in his balls. His scrotum contracted and rasped against itself. He shuddered; he was getting hard in his spandex suit, and the cameras took in every pulsing detail. He tried numbing his erection through breathing exercises, but his cock refused to cooperate; every swollen vein pressed against his skin tight suit.

Primacy's chrome rod of control suddenly chimed, and the evil mastermind checked the computer gadget on his arm that gave him bio readouts. His brows furrowed; he was trying to understand what the data was telling him; his eyes widened.

Stalwart struggled harder, desperate to fight this humiliation and more eager to surrender to it, but his muscles were locked, and the helplessness of it all sent a spasm through his prick. A spot cooled against the pulsing skin of his shaft. He was leaking precum. His heart was pounding in delight as his mind raced through worst-case scenarios. Everyone was staring at him, exposed, vulnerable.

Cautiously, Primacy went to one knee and inspected Stalwart's erection. A smirk crept across his lips. "Really?" he whispered, his tone one of delighted mischief. "Imagine that. All that power, and your desperate to be my little toy."

Stalwart moaned and Primacy smiled. "I had something planned, but this ... this is more fun. Your safeword is pineapple," he whispered.

"What?"

"'Pineapple.' Nice and loud for the cameras."

The crowd gasped when Primacy stood and pulled his pecker out. People shouted in indignation, and television censors raced to blur his uncut manhood in its full glory, the skin pale, the foreskin pinched above a swollen head, the member six inches soft.

Stalwart's heartbeat pounded, and Primacy smiled, his fingers gently pulling his foreskin back and forth, teasing glimpses at the one-eye wet with a salty pearl of precum. Was he going to ejaculate on Stalwart, force him to fellate him? Stalwart gasped; deep down, he needed to know the flavor of Primacy's fluids. If he struggled a little bit, he could pretend he didn't want to sample his rival's manhood and nobody would suspect a thing.

Afterward, he could vanish from the public eye for a few months for a much-needed vacation, and return darker and edgier and with a new nickname. He'd been struggling to find a way to rebrand himself, to become more elusive and less in the public eye, and this was a perfect opportunity.

Primacy began pissing on him.

It was sudden. Unexpected. Stalwart froze. Hot piss waterfalled from his lips, salty and tasting sharply of vitamin B. The audience screamed out in shock, and the stadium shook to its foundations, and yet all Stalwart could hear was the soft patter of piss as it struck his head.

He almost cried Pineapple, but then he understood the diabolical plan.

A safe word was complicity in the act, and that made him even harder, bathed in another man's urine and unwilling to fight.

"Take it," Primacy said, raising his chrome rod and with it, Stalwart's head. The stream hit his open mouth. He swallowed. He didn't fight it anymore. He was tired of being in control, being a spotless hero. His eyes met Primacy's chestnut gaze, but not with any act of defiance. His demure peeping came from under his eyebrows, in supplication. He wasn't broken; he was desperately willing.

When Primacy finished pissing, he slapped his cock against Stalwart's face and whispered, "Let me help you with that." He pulled a strange-looking red tipped pen from his utility belt and ran it along Stalwart's bulge; the spandex split open, Stalwart's cock popping loose. It was engorged. Precum dripped on the AstroTurf. Primacy flicked a switch on the chrome rod and muscles around the base of Stalwart's manhood contracted in desperate pulses.

Stalwart whimpered; the contractions were milking his cock, slow and steady. There was no tenderness to it, and the mechanical sensation of being treated like cattle pulled him deeper into helpless, blissful submission.

"Good boy," Primacy whispered, his voice thick. Primacy was hard now; his pecker arched like a scimitar; his foreskin half-pulled over its exposed head. The stadium roared in anger and sympathy for Stalwart, but it wasn't a sympathy he needed or wanted.

Primacy grabbed the sides of Stalwart's head and slid his cock into his open mouth. The fat head brushed against the roof of his soft palate and past the tonsils. Stalwart struggled not to gag, and with another press of the chrome rod, Primacy lowered the gag reflex so they could have a bit more fun. Stalwart brushed his tongue under Primacy's manhood, and Primacy stiffened. Stalwart could geld him, they both knew it, but Stalwart pressed hard enough with his lips to squeeze out a jerk of piss that was thick with precum. Primacy moaned softly and smothered Stalwart's nose into his black bush before building up to a jackhammer tempo. The deep thrusts coated Primacy's shaft in slick throat spit.

He grunted hard, moaned.

The contractions on Stalwart's cock increased in tempo, building him toward the inevitable ejaculation.

"I'm ... going to ... cum," Stalwart gagged out the words.

"Do it, slut," Primacy grunted.

"No—" Stalwart said, mumbling with a cock in his mouth, struggling not to cum ... yet, "cum—explosive!"

Primacy's eyes widened and he threw himself to the side.

Stalwart's balls contracted hard and his cock hammered out an orbital strike of an ejaculation. He came at Mach 10, shredding AstroTurf to ribbons and throwing up a cloud of sand and displacing stones from a 155mm-sized artillery crater.

Stalwart trembled on spent limbs, panting as the stones rained down and the dust cloud shrouded them both from the cameras.

"Not the direction I thought I'd take this character," Primacy told him, "but now I'm the worst villain they've seen." He kissed Stalwart under cover of dust, a gesture that spoke of love and promises. "Next month, I'll be robbing Stallion Enterprises. FYI, it's a trap." He winked.

"I'll be ready," Stalwart said.

"So will I," Primacy said, showing him the chrome rod, "just as soon as I reconfigure this for more ... functionality."

Before the dust could settle, people were already crowding the aisles in their dash to escape. Primacy was already gone, vanished through an energy aperture that severed his control over Stalwart and the crowd. Stalwart tucked his half-hard cock back into the slit in his uniform and tasted the precum that glazed his fingertips before taking to the air.

The next few weeks would be charged with speculation, but he would remain the victim in this episode. They'd search for their hero, beg him to come out of hiding and show him an outpouring of love, never realizing that their love and adoration wasn't what comforted him. What he needed, he wouldn't find in the spotlight; what he needed were those moments when he could surrender to a control rod and be someone's sub.

MECHANOGENATION

BY KONSTANTINE PARADIAS

SHE PURRS, EVER SO SLIGHTLY UNDER ME as we speed across the interstate, and I know that she wants me.

Jittery like a schoolboy, I check the stretch of empty road around us, squint against the moonlit landscape around us. A tiny sedan speeds by and I catch a glimpse of a woman's flushed face, her crotch pressed up against the gear stick.

She huffs again, and I hear the soft, *hissing* noise she makes as she unfolds herself around me. I adjust my rearview mirror and the leather folds of the backseat part, revealing the off-gray flesh of her, her glistening bloom, slick with her juices. Her nub slowly pops out from the top, her little crown jewel.

"I'm coming back there," I tell her and I feel the wheel freezing up in my hands, feel the gas slowly depress from under me as we gently pick up speed and swerve. It's her little way of foreplay, the little nudge she gave me for years before I decided to finally give in to her.

143

Pushing back the passenger seat, I climb back and sit beside her opening, my fingers tracing the outline of her lips. Her engine revs as I feel her reacting to me, watch her folds blossom outward, slick with juices but I take my time, circling her nub with two fingers, trailing around it, watching it grow with anticipation. I dip one thumb inside her and hook it in, savoring the wet, sucking sound she makes as she clenches around my finger.

"Whoa, give it time," I say, teasing. She gently swerves into the fast lane, her little way of forcing my hand. I just smile and slip two fingers deeper inside her, tease her nub and prop it up so I can suck it. Her taste is cool, almost minty. Inside, she is burning hot.

Slowly, I pull down my pants and place myself across her. A station wagon passes, and I can see a horrified man staring at my half-naked body, my member sliding across her nub and all I can do is laugh. She doesn't even bother to honk at him, just zooms past him the second she feels me slide into her.

"Goddamn," I groan as I plunge myself inside her, as I feel her grip me in her hot insides, her folds quivering against me. I lay across her and grind deeply, feeling her grip me, feeling the seat under me depress, but I buck up against her, grind up into her and feel her squirt her wiper fluid around me, easing my motions.

My fingers still tease her nub, feel it grow in my hand, and I tease it, feeling it grow, up across my chest, to my mouth. I put it in my mouth without even thinking and run circles the tip with my tongue, suck at the tip. She stalls on the fast lane, and a semi blares at us angrily as it passes us by. I doubt she even notices. My hands tease her extended nub, and I can feel her milk running up across the length, spurting into my mouth. I drink it all down even as I thrust into her, grinding deep inside her, feeling my release and hers building up.

"Do it. Do it now," I groan. She holds on to me until the last second then pops the backseat compartment, reveals her clanking

144

red interior in a hiss of smoke. I release into the jumbled machinery, into the crashing, clanking pistons, into the hissing leather womb, aiming for the funnel at the center. Some of my blow splashes across the hot metal surface, and I watch it bubble and boil, a million little soldiers dying in a bubbling holocaust. A few spurts make it inside, dripping into the machinery, sucked into her crucible. I watch it churn for a while, watch the pumps and pistons work their magic, watch her womb depress and slowly grow and I know it's taken.

"How long, baby?" I ask her. She just revs her engine. Not too long. They're coming faster now. I take the wheel and take the next exit, gun it across a sheer climb, toward the mountain path that led to the old Make Out point. The place is still littered with scattered mounds of beer cans and used rubbers. The stripped carcass of Mackie's old Toyota still lays at the bottom of the gorge. Its glove compartment has turned into a mausoleum for emperor rats.

I park her across an ancient skid mark trail and run back to her trunk. She shudders and shivers now, getting closer. Her exhaust pumps out a cloud of smoke, and she growls as her payload reaches its full size. She never let me look inside, so I can only imagine it: the tearing leather, the machinery clanking back to make room for it, its body clanging up against the trunk as it stretches ....

"Easy now baby, easy now ..." I tell her and her trunk pops, just a little bit, releasing a burst of lukewarm juices and motor oil. I pull it up slowly and look down, at the tiny thing in her insides, the little rectangular creature that cry-honks into the night, its headlight-eyes glowing so bright that they almost blind me.

I help it out into the world, cradling the soft, yielding flesh stretched out across the rigid metal insides. Its pliable little wheels spin against me, leaving sticky little tire-marks across my shirt. When I let it down, it starts to rev and turn and drive circles by itself, as playful as a colt. We watch it spin and turn and speed across Make Out point, its windowpanes growing across its frame even as I watch. Within a week, it will have grown its own seat cushions. It'll be out on the prowl by the end of the month, so long as it can find a driver to take care of it.

"You take care now, you hear?" I call for it, but it's too busy speeding around itself, honking at the moon, chasing after its own headlight trail. Used to be, we would herd them together, but their roughhousing would get to be too much. Within a day, they'd become so territorial, they would wipe each other out entirely. So now, we give them room to grow, driving away as soon as they're out and about.

"Come on, sweetheart. Off we go," I tell her and drive back slowly, sneaking glances back at the headlight trail, listening for the distant engine sounds, the playful honking. I try to think of how it's going to turn out: the color of its chassis, the tint in its headlights, the pitch of its horn. Beneath me, I can feel her revving uneasily, eager to get back on the road. I pat her panel and softly whisper sweet nothings to her as we make our way back to the interstate.

In the cold, dark hours before the dawn, I see a car speeding by in the fast lane, its passengers howling as they're caught in the throes of ecstasy, and I know it will be all right.

PLEASE

BY CASSANDRA KHAW

OU'RE STICKY," SHE SAID WITH A LILT of surprise, half-laughing.

"Can't help it. This is a somewhat stimulating situa— ow."

"What did I say about sass?"

"Yes, miss." He sighs into her hair, breathing her, fingers digging into her thigh. A smell of honey and rosewater, a hint of the afternoon's sweat. "What are you doing?"

"What does it look like I'm doing?"

"Nothing appropriate for the venue, certainly."

She laughs against his ear, teeth grazing the lobe. "What a clever boy."

"Madame, I am not your dog."

Her hold tightens, slides upwards, thumb rubbing circles across his tip. "You're not. Puppy, maybe. An overgrown, overeager puppy."

He considers the compromise. "I can live with that."

Faster now, her strokes, each pass culminating in a gentle squeeze. "You have to tell me when you're getting close."

It takes him a moment to form a reply, his breath rasping. "Alright."

"*Good* boy."

"I wish you'd stop—"

"Do you?"

"No. Not really." He shivers. "Close. I—"

"The bar?"

"No. I—You know what I'm trying to say, you minx."

"Mm." Her tongue slides behind his ear, a wet warmth.

"Closer."

"Mmm."

He swallows. It's becoming harder to think. "Are you really planning to have me—"

"Mmm."

"That's still not an answer."

"Oh, I know."

"I don't know why I put up with—" His voice catches into a hiss. "Would you at least consider finding some tissue or something?"

"Maybe."

"There is going to be a mess."

"Mmm."

"I wish you'd just use your words."

She slides the fingers of her spare hand along his lower lip before rapping at his teeth with a nail. He parts his mouth obligingly. "What did I tell you about yours?"

"Pardon?" Unable to resist, he licks at her fingertips.

"Only asked you to tell me when you were getting close. I didn't say anything about the wisecracking."

"Part of the—"

"Do I have to use my mouth there before you'll focus?"

He whimpers aloud this time.

"Good boy."

This time, he doesn't argue, rocking against her grip, all pretenses of decorum gone.

"Very, very close now."

"How close?"

"Cataclysmically close." He swallows. "Please."

"Please what?"

"I need—"

"You need?"

"May I—"

"May you what?"

An animal voice escapes, desperate. "I—"

"Are you asking for permission to climax? That'd be messy, though. No towels. No tissue. No discreet route to the bathroom. Where do you expect to deposit the outcome? Did you want me to *swallow* it?" Her fingers stilled.

He whines at the image. "Whatever is—whatever works for you."

Her grin is incandescent as she withdraws her hand. "Good to know. You should probably pull yourself back together, by the way. We are expecting people."

"I hate you."

"No. No, you don't."

"No, I don't."

TO ME, 'NASTY' IS AN EXPLICITLY OPPOSITIONAL CONDITION. IT PRESUPPOSES SOMETHING THAT IS NOT NASTY BY WHICH TO COMPARE ITSELF. THE CLEAN. THE PROPER. THE REGIMENTED. NASTY, IN THAT CASE, REFERS TO ANYTHING THAT CHALLENGES THE SUPREMACY OF SOCIAL, ECONOMIC, AND PERSONAL PRESCRIPTION. IT'S A SORT OF CELEBRATORY ACT OF SABOTAGE, THE CONSTRUCTION OF SOCIAL STRUCTURES THAT EXIST OUTSIDE OF THE STATUS QUO. IT CAN BE (AND OFTEN IS) SEXUAL BUT DOESN'T NEED TO BE. IT'S A WILLINGNESS TO EMBRACE EMPOWERING PRACTICES, NOT JUST IN SPITE OF THE SCORN POWERFUL PEOPLE HOLD FOR THOSE PRACTICES BUT AS A WEAPON WIELDED AGAINST THOSE PEOPLE.

D. F. WARRICK

The Things I Told the Cops After the Uprising (and a Few Things I Wish I'd Told Them)

by D.F. Warrick

M? AH. THAT'S A HARD QUESTION TO ANSWER. She's ... I'm not sure I've ever not known her. I can tell you when I first noticed her. But when I met her?

"Okay, yes, that's ... I'm being esoteric, it's ... Rissa makes it look so cool. So I attend a support group thing. Wednesday nights. We meet at this café, a bunch of us, and we talk. How HRT's going. How dating while trans is a fucking nightmare ... it's ... I dunno ... it's helpful, sometimes.

Talking.

"What did I say about sass?"

I was there, and I was listening to this girl talk about her pussy.

Saying, "Nobody can tell me I have a cock. It's mine. I can call it what I want. I design its nature, and it complies." God, I hated her. I mean, she's really sweet, really supportive, just the best, but my god, I hated her. She's beautiful, okay? She looks in the mirror and sees herself. I know she does. Me? I look down at myself in the shower, past these desperate little tits, and see my cock. This inarguable little reminder that I had a different name once. That I occupied a different space. I know I should have felt empowered, should have taken her ability to reinvent her anatomy through—what—repurposing vocabulary, I guess—I should have taken that as a signal that I was capable of the same sort of thing, but I couldn't. I could only hear her words as a brag. "I'm such a good trans girl. I don't even think of my cock as a cock. How about you, Robin? No? Oh, that's too bad. Are you sure you're in the right group?"

And I'm thinking all of this shit as I walk out of the café and onto the street, as I light up a cigarette and wonder if I'm walking too much like a man, smoking too much like a man, living too much like a man, and then there's this girl next to me. And she ... takes my hand and tucks it under her arm, guides my fingers around her elbow. It was ... walking with someone like that, holding onto the crook of their arm, it feels ... I just held on. Just walked. And as we walked, her name came to me like I'd known it for a long time. Rissa. Born inside my memories. Hatched. She said, "I love it when you do your hair like that," and leaned her head against my shoulder, and I realized we were in love. Had been in love for a while. "You're so fucking pretty, Robin. It's ridonkulous. Let's get you home, yeah?"

Ooh! Good photo! She looks a little like Ali standing over Frasier, don't you think? Whoever took it, they must have snapped it right after the guy crumpled. You can't see how badly he was bleeding in this, but Rissa told me she opened him up pretty hardcore. I didn't see her grab the brick. She slipped away from me, and I was suddenly surrounded by all these protesters. I used to hate it when she would do that. Slip away and leave me surrounded by strangers, wondering which of them were staring at me, whether they could see the stubble peeking through my foundation. Lefties can be funny about trans stuff. All these passionate anarcho-whatevers, standing up against oppressive hierarchies, but artificial gender hierarchies apparently aren't sufficiently oppressive. You're still allowed to find the tranny icky.

All I saw was those big muscular skinhead boys standing in front of the gym with their arms crossed. Throwing up sig-heils. Trying to find the best flexing posture to show off their fucking "eighty-eight" tattoos. They can't help themselves. Like, we all heard they'd kind of occupied the boxing gym, so we were going to be there one way or the other, but they didn't have to stand outside like, "Yep! We're Nazis! Check out our big Nazi boxing gym! Did we mention we're Nazis?" Ugh. One of them—iron cross throat tattoo, patchy red beard—screamed in the face of the guy at the front of the line: "Diversity equals white genocide!" Fucking parrot-squawk philosophy. Inherited.

Okay, so then ... Rissa is no longer holding her brick. It's airborne, and then it's skull-borne, and then it clatters onto the asphalt. The red-bearded Nazi falls, throws his hands over his head, bleeds, like I told you. Like she told me. I see her then, with her fists held at her sides, her mouth open, snarling like Ali. And she says ... oof ... she says, "I fucking wish!"

Of course, after Rissa bricked that piece of shit, everything exploded. One second, it's all rhetorical, you know? And then Rissa. Rissa the event. Rissa the verb. And everybody kind of ... got permission. A big brawl like that, it feels like a savage party. The weird smell of sweat eating its way out from under deodorant and perfume. The way you press against all these strangers while somehow remaining intimate and expressive with the person you're dancing with. It's ... I mean, HRT has changed the way I experience ... stuff, but ... but watching her, watching Rissa kick the shit out of those boneheads, it's ... it was ... I was ... hard, I guess, but I didn't feel hard.

I felt wet.

Hm. Hahaha. Oh wow. You guys got a lot of good pictures of her that night, didn't you? Traffic cam? Yes, that's Rissa. God, she's like ... she's really going to town on that car, huh? How much did that cost, you guys?

I don't remember the riot as a sequence of discrete events. I remember sirens, running from you guys. I remember how we went from running to marching like the two were natural stages of the same metamorphosis. I remember setting fires. Garbage cans. Broken windows. I remember Rissa in this picture. On top of the cruiser, bringing that fence post down on the wind shield. I remember my skin feeling hot, my scalp tingling. I remember ...

So look. Look at this picture. There's Rissa, yeah? Fucking up your cruiser. Okay, now look ... I guess I'd be .... there. Yes. There I am. See? Who's next to me? Hm? Who is leaning in to whisper something in my ear? Can you tell?

Maybe ... maybe cities have ghosts? Maybe they spawn a sort of ... a vengeful spirit. Or maybe ... maybe communities produce antibodies. Little white blood cells that incite swelling and chip away at the structures that break us and hurt us and isolate us. Maybe that's ... I believe that's what Rissa is.

Rissa whispered "I have an idea," while I watched Rissa wreck your cruiser. "Such an idea. Oh, Robin, I have the greatest idea." She coiled her fingers around mine, and dragged me away from her, toward her, until we were hidden in this little alcove next to the basement entrance of ... I dunno, someplace. She kissed me. And maybe that was the first time we'd ever kissed, I don't know, but it felt like the hundredth. Time and sequence are weird with

Rissa. God, we were starving for each other. I felt her hand snake beneath my skirt. I felt her tug my gaff to the side, gasped, stole air from her mouth. Her fingers brush against my ... I don't ... you know what, fuck it. Right then, at that moment, with people shouting and chanting within earshot, with your boys shouting orders into megaphones, with the sky turning orange above us, I had complete authority over my anatomy. I could have and be whatever I wanted. So ... my pussy. No. I felt her fingers brush against my cunt. Oh, I like that. I like saying that. I like believing it.

Soon she had her skirt hiked up, her panties dangling around one ankle, my panties down around my knees, and I was inside of her, and she was inside of me, and ... and I swear that at that moment, her skin was ... wet asphalt. The glass of every skyscraper in her hair. I saw her sprawling in every direction, felt her fingers traveling up my spine like subway cars down a track, saw her veins turn to sewer tunnels and saw her eyes turn to lamp posts.

So ... even if you found her, what do you think you'd do to her? Charge her with assault? With destruction of property? Throw handcuffs on her and throw her in a cell? Please. It's taken centuries for men to tie her up, and she's still breaking free. And those of us who love her, those of us who are loved by her? Well ... burning a city is like ... it's like stripping off its clothes. Finding the bare body it wants to have underneath. Loving that body. Fucking it. No cocks, no cunts, just ... us. Just home. Unencumbered. Naked.

THE STRAW MAN

BY JESSICA FREELY

*Y*OU EVER NOTICE HOW THE MOST VIRULENTLY ANTI-GAY LEADERS always seem to wind up in bed with male prostitutes?

It's no coincidence. Nobody gets that passionate without a personal connection.

I should know. I was once the biggest homophobe preacher who ever crawled out of Billy Graham's asshole, and I'd still be calling Hellfire and damnation down on the gays every Sunday and fucking men every Saturday if I hadn't got caught. And you know what? The moment my spunk hit our organist in the eye? That's when I was truly *born again.*

On my knees before Jesus Christ Our Savior and Jimmy Tingle of Fayetteville, the light of God's love sprayed down on me, bathing me clean and pure as the day I was born.

I haven't come that hard since.

But one thing still gets me close.

Mike's new suit is too tight. He shifts in his seat but can't get comfortable.

Now that he's taken office, every Republican on the Hill wants in on his weekly Bible-study group. The room is packed. The air is warm and ripe with the musk of strong, clean, Christian male bodies.

It reminds him of the man in the *Sbarro's* restroom in Breezewood last summer.

Tall, unshaven, dressed like a trucker but not an ounce of paunch on him, he leaned against a stall door and stroked his cock.

The smell in the Bible-study room grows stronger. Mike fights for breath but his tie constricts around his neck. Thank goodness Ryan's giving the introductory reading today.

"Do you not know that your bodies are members of Christ Himself? Shall I then take the members of Christ and unite them with a prostitute?"

That's what Ryan chooses? Corinthians? Members and prostitutes? Mike almost misses the response. "Never!" he shouts a fraction of a second after everyone else. He's got to pull it together. It's his turn.

He stands. "And so we must refrain from any union with those immoral libertines on the opposite side of the aisle. They will stop at nothing to further their Godless agenda. Emboldening the gays and the atheists—men with no regard for the sanctity of their own souls, let alone anyone else's."

The trucker's smile uncoiled like the Serpent from the Tree. Dark eyes mesmerized Mike with promises of secrecy. He knew he should leave, but he'd been on the campaign trail for weeks and his balls were bluer than a Washtenaw County election map.

"Hanging out in bus stations," Mike says, "loitering in men's rooms, heedless of the word of God or anything else except bending another man over, yanking his pants down—"

The whole Bible study group rises to its feet.

"—and violating him!" It's hotter than ever but Mike doesn't care. His suit feels like it's about to break open like a chrysalis, releasing him from his earthly shackles of sin. "Over and over again!"

The trucker circled slowly, so close their shoulders brushed. The hard touch of muscle riveted Mike to the spot.

"Stuffing his virginal, Christian asshole with Devil dick!"

The trucker stopped right behind Mike. Strong hands gripped his shoulders, and a lean, firm body pressed against his back.

"No!" cries Ryan. "Lord preserve us from Devil Dick!"

Ignoring the interruption, Mike continues, "Pinning his wrists to the mirror with one hand while covering his mouth with the other!"

"To prevent his righteous cries!" Ryan is trying to steal the spotlight.

Mike won't let that happen. "Assaulting his body and his morals until he begs to be released."

"Until he'd gladly vote for election reform if he could just reach his constituency!"

Dammit, Ryan. "But he can't. The nation has deserted him! His people have abandoned the righteous path!"

Stubble scratched Mike's neck. Hot breath caressed his ear. "When you're ready."

"I-I-"

Ryan exhorts the crowd, "Are we going to let that happen?"

"No!" Their voices are deafening. "Never!"

The trucker slid a folded scrap of paper in the breast pocket of Mike's shirt and walked away.

Never.

Later Mike sits in his office. The guest list for his birthday party glows on his monitor. The event will be held at his official residence at the Naval Observatory, a select gathering—just a hundred or so of his closest campaign contributors and a handful of press from the lifestyle segments.

In his lap, he folds and unfolds the *Sbarro's* receipt. The cheap, high clay-content paper slips between his fingers like the petals of a flower, falling apart under his touch, tearing at the creases.

But the phone number on the back is still legible.

He can't.

His suit is too tight. He can't even reach his keyboard to add one more guest. And he can't reach the wastebasket to throw the number away, either.

What is wrong with him, letting some ... idle notion paralyze him with indecision? Is this the behavior of the Vice President of the United States of America? Is he a man? Where is his faith in God and in himself?

Mike forces himself to stand. He unbuttons his jacket. Why not just call?

The number won't be active anymore. The trucker won't answer, and if he does he won't accept the invitation. This isn't the sort of thing someone like him would enjoy. It's not the sort of thing anyone enjoys, really. Besides, he's a working man. He'll be busy.

And so what if the man accepts? Mike will just introduce him as a regular *Joe-the-Plumber* he met on the campaign trail. Which is entirely true. It's not like he intends to drag the man down to Dick Cheney's secret underground bunker or anything.

Mike loosens his tie and takes a sip of water.

It is his birthday party. He can invite anyone he wants. In fact, the only reason not to would be if his faith is too weak to withstand the temptation of ... no. That's not right either. There is no temptation because he harbors no lustful thoughts about men.

None.

He'll prove it.

If anything, the trucker's even more attractive in a tux.

No. That's not what Mike means. Just that he looks ... sophisticated. The sharp lines of the suit frame his body, wrapping it in an elegance that at once disguises and enhances his power.

Mike downs the last of his champagne and bubbles sizzle in his sinuses. He dashes for the bathroom before he sprays all over his guests.

This is a mistake. He committed hubris, pitting his will against Satan's tricks. Because that's what the trucker is: a temptation straight from Hell. Mike needs to find Ryan and have a Bible study session. Right now.

But he can't.

"You okay?"

Mike straightens from the sink, and there he is, standing in the open doorway. The moment is so like their first meeting. Like being in two places at once. "It's late. I didn't think you'd come."

The trucker may have cleaned up well, but that slow smile is still filthy. "I was curious about the place. I've never been to a Naval Observatory before."

"Would you like a ... tour of the house?"

"Is it true what Biden said about Cheney building an underground bunker here?"

Mike can't hold back a grin. He's hard as the rock of St. Peter but he doesn't care. It feels good, natural. "You've heard about that?"

"I did a little Googling."

"Well, we'll have to see." Mike lets his grin turn teasing and leads the way through the dining room into the kitchen. He knows exactly where they're going and why.

If he's honest with himself, he's known all along.

It's true. He has committed the sin of hubris. All these years, he pretended to know how God made him and for what purpose.

His suits don't fit. How can they when they're cut for the man he expected himself to be, the man the country expected him to be, but not the man God made him? This wasn't his decision now. Not really. It was God's. And God would decide if this would be a private matter or a public one.

Mike pauses on the threshold of the bunker, the gleaming metal of the door cold against his palm. His heart thunders inside him like a galloping horde of the righteous host.

The trucker stands two paces away, watching, silent. Most of the press has gone home, but a few of the hungrier ones still linger. The tabloid sort that might take the opportunity to poke around. Just the type to have a camera ready.

It probably wouldn't happen.

But it could.

His whole life. Everything his parents taught him, everything he taught his own children. Not to mention his career. All of it balanced against a few moments with this stranger, and he already knows he'll take the risk.

Why?

That is God's mystery. All these months he's secretly blamed the trucker for pushing him over some irrevocable line between righteousness and sin, but that's not how God's love works, is it? God is all knowing and all forgiving.

All this time Mike's tried to hide the truth with self-denial. But he's in God's hands now, as in truth he always has been. "The lock doesn't work."

In the dim light of the bare bulb above them the trucker's eyes gleam. "Trust me. It's better this way."

Mike takes his hand and they cross the threshold together.

THE AUTHORS OF
NASTY

Cassie Alexander

Cassie Alexander is the author of the *Edie Spence* urban fantasy series, *Nightshifted et al,* out now through St. Martin's Press, and the very hot paranormal *Sleeping with Monster* series and the *Dark Ink Tattoo* series.

Matthew F. Amati

Matthew F. Amati was born in Chicago Heights, IL. His intimate friends call him "Candle Ends" and his enemies "Toasted Cheese." He has a blog; it's this one: www.mattamati.com

Steve Berman

Steve Berman has sold over a hundred articles, essays, and short stories, most of the latter being queer speculative and young adult fiction. The rarest thing he has even consumed is fermented mare's milk in Outer Mongolia. He enjoyed it. He hails from New

Jersey, the only state in the union with an official devil. Later in 2017, his newest short story collection, *Fit for Consumption*, gay horror tales that involve food and men and various hungers will be published by Lethe Press.

〜 ? 〜

Robert Brouhard

Robert Brouhard is a member of the Horror Writers Association, Assistant Editor for *Cemetery Dance Magazine*, and a family man.

〜 ? 〜

'Nathan Burgoine

'Nathan Burgoine lives in Ottawa with his husband Daniel and a rescued husky, Coach. His previous erotic short fiction appears in *Tented, Blood Sacraments, Wings, Erotica Exotica, Afternoon Pleasures, Riding the Rails, Dirty Diner, Sweat, The Biggest Lover, and Threesome: Him, Him,* and *Me.* He has also written two novels, *Light* (a Lambda Literary Finalist), and *Triad Blood.* He rarely wears a mask. Find him online at nathanburgoine.com.

〜 ? 〜

Tom Cardamone

Tom Cardamone is the author of the Lambda Literary Award-winning speculative novella *Green Thumb* and the erotic fantasy novel *The Werewolves of Central Park* as well as the novella *Pacific Rimming.* His short story collection, *Pumpkin Teeth*, was a finalist for the Lambda Literary Award and Black Quill Award. Additionally, he has edited *The Lost Library: Gay Fiction Rediscovered* and the anthology *Lavender Menace: Tales of Queer Villainy!*, which was nominated for the Over The Rainbow List by the LGBT Round Table of the American Library Association. Lambda Literary described his 2016 collection, *Night Sweats: Tales of Homosexual Wonder and Woe*, as "a heady mix of subtle, understated wonder, unmitigated horror, and powerful eroticism, with

each story working its individual magic on the reader."
His short stories have appeared in numerous anthologies and
magazines, some of which have been collected on his website
http://www.pumpkinteeth.net.

Ann Castle

Ann Castle lives in central Illinois, surrounded by corn. She
spends as much time as possible outdoors, growing vegetables or
removing invasive plants from local parks. She loves trees, but
not in that way.

Darien Cox

Author of gay mystery/scifi series *THE VILLAGE*, Darien Cox
enjoys using romantic and erotic fiction to explore the intensity,
insanity, humor, and chaos that accompanies cupid's arrow. His
author site is DarienCox.com

Rose de Fer

Rose de Fer's stories have appeared in numerous anthologies including *Best Women's Erotica*, *Best Lesbian Erotica*, and *The Mam-
moth Book of Erotic Romance & Domination*. Her gothic werewolf
story "Snowlight, Moonlight" opens the highly regarded anthology *Red Velvet & Absinthe*. Her novella *Lust Ever After* (Mischief
Books) is a kinky re-imagining of Bride of Frankenstein. Other
stories appear in *Darker Edge of Desire*, *A Princess Bound*, *Hungry
for More*, *The Big Book of Submission*, and many other Mischief
anthologies including *Underworlds*, *Submission* and *Forever Bound*.
She lives in England.

Gemma Files

Former film critic turned award-winning horror author Gemma Files is probably best-known for her Weird Western *Hexslinger* Series (*A Book of Tongues, A Rope of Thorns* and *A Tree of Bones,* all from ChiZine Publications). Her most recent book, *Experimental Film,* won both the 2015 Shirley Jackson Award for Best Novel and the 2015 Sunburst Award for Best Novel (Adult). She is hard at work on her next project.

Jessica Freely

Jessica Freely is a best-selling author of queer science fiction and romance with over twenty years of experience writing, publishing, and teaching genre fiction. She began her career writing science fiction under her legal name, Anne Harris. Her first novel, *The Nature of Smoke,* made the shortlist for the Sense of Gender Award for feminist science fiction in Japanese translation and her second, *Accidental Creatures,* won the Spectrum Award for LGBTQ science fiction. She was also a Nebula finalist with her fantasy humor short story, "Still Life with Boobs." As Pearl North she published the *Libyrinth* trilogy of young adult science fiction novels and became a Norton Award finalist with the second book, *The Boy from Ilysies.* Since 2008, Freely has published over ten gay and gender-queer romance novels and novellas, many of them bestsellers in the science fiction and paranormal subgenres. She has mentored graduate students in Seton Hill University's Writing Popular Fiction MFA program since 2007.

Lazuli Jones

Lazuli Jones' particular brand of erotica has previously appeared in *Best Women's Erotica of the Year, Volume 1,* as well as Torquere Press' *They Do* and *Mythologically Torqued* anthologies. Her first novel, *Abyssal Zone,* is available from eXtasy Books. A performer and queer activist, Lazuli lives in southern Ontario with her partner.

✎ ⸮ ✎

Cassandra Khaw

Cassandra Khaw writes horror, press releases, video games, articles about video games, and tabletop RPGs. These are not necessarily unrelated items. Her work can be found in professional short story magazines such as *Clarkesworld, Fireside Fiction, Uncanny,* and *Shimmer.* Cassandra's first original novella, *Hammers on Bone,* came out in October 2016 from Tor.com. To her mild surprise, people seem to enjoy it. She occasionally spends time in a Muay Thai gym punching people and pads.

✎ ⸮ ✎

Selena Kitt

Selena Kitt is a NEW YORK TIMES bestselling and award-winning author of erotic and romance fiction. She is one of the highest selling erotic writers in the business with over two million books sold!

Her writing embodies everything from the spicy to the scandalous, but watch out-this kitty also has sharp claws and her stories often include intriguing edges and twists that take readers to new, thought-provoking depths.

When she's not pawing away at her keyboard, Selena runs an innovative publishing company (excessica.com) and bookstore (excitica.com), as well as two erotica and erotic romance promotion companies (excitesteam.com and and excitespice.com) and she now runs the Erotica Readers and Writers Association.

Her books *EcoErotica* (2009), *The Real Mother Goose* (2010) and **Heidi and the Kaiser** (2011) were all Epic Award Finalists. Her only gay male romance, *Second Chance,* won the Epic Award in Erotica in 2011. Her story, *Connections,* was one of the runners-up

167

for the 2006 Rauxa Prize, given annually to an erotic short story of "exceptional literary quality."

Her book, *Babysitting the Baumgartners*, is now an adult film by Adam & Eve, starring Mick Blue, Anikka Albrite, Sara Luvv and A.J. Applegate.

She can be reached on her website at www.selenakitt.com

Konstantine Paradias

Konstantine Paradias is a writer by choice. His short stories have been published in the *AE Canadian Science Fiction Review*, *The Curious Gallery Magazine*, and *the BATTLE ROYALE Slambook* by Haikasoru. His short story, "How You Ruined Everything" has been included in Tangent Online's 2013 recommended SF reading list and his short story "The Grim" has been nominated for a Pushcart Prize.

Charles Payseur

Charles Payseur is an avid reader, writer, and reviewer of all things speculative. His fiction and poetry have appeared at *Strange Horizons, Lightspeed Magazine, The Book Smugglers,* and many more. He runs Quick Sip Reviews, contributes as short fiction specialist at Nerds of a Feather, Flock Together, and can be found drunkenly reviewing *Goosebumps* on his Patreon. You can find him gushing about short fiction (and occasionally his cats) on Twitter as @ClowderofTwo.

Nathan Pettigrew

Nathan Pettigrew was born and raised near New Orleans, and lives with his pet rabbits in the Tampa Bay area. His story "Dog Killer" was named among the Top 4 Winners and Finalists of the

Writer's Digest 8th annual Popular Fiction Awards for the Crime category, and appears in *State of Horror: Louisiana Vol. II.* Other stories are featured through the award-winning pages of *Thuglit,* and *DarkMedia Original Fiction and Poetry.* Visit Nathan at Solarcide.com, or on Twitter @NathanBorn2010.

🙌 ? 🙌

Kaysee Renee Robichaud

Kaysee Renee Robichaud has a fascination with stitchery, but not quite to an extent matching the protagonist in her story. She is the author of several short stories for publishers like *Cleis Press, Ravenous Romance, Circlet,* and more. She looks forward to seeing new adventures of her m/m gangsters (*Private Loves of Public Enemies*), polyamorous starship crew (*Dragonfly Chronicles*), and Lovecraftian book sleuths (*Bookworm Brigade*) find their way into bookstores this year. Under another name, she has been penning G.I. Joe stories for the Kindle Worlds program. Her current favorite is *Cover Girl: By Any Other Name.* A *Baroness* novel is coming soon because: The Baroness! If you want to keep up with her antics, check out her highly unpredictable and even more highly irregular blog at: kayseerenee.livejournal.com.

🙌 ? 🙌

Kelly Robson

Kelly Robson lives in Toronto with her wife, fellow SF writer A.M. Dellamonica. Kelly's novella "Waters of Versailles" won the 2016 Aurora Award, and in 2016, she was a finalist for the Nebula Award, World Fantasy Award, Theodore Sturgeon Award, and Sunburst Award. She is currently a finalist for the John W. Campbell Award for Best New Writer. Kelly's time travel novella "Gods, Monsters, and the Lucky Peach" will be published by Tor.com imprint in 2018.

🙌 ? 🙌

Jason S. Ridler

Jason S. Ridler is a writer, improv actor, and historian. He is the author of *A TRIUMPH FOR SAKURA, BLOOD AND SAWDUST,* the *Spar Battersea* thrillers and the upcoming BRIMSTONE FILES series for Nightshade Press. He's also published over sixty-five stories in such magazines and anthologies as T*he Big Click, Beneath Ceaseless Skies, Out of the Gutter,* and more. He also writes the column FXXK WRITING! for **Flash Fiction Online.** A former punk rock musician and cemetery groundskeeper, Mr. Ridler holds a Ph.D. in War Studies from the Royal Military College of Canada. He lives in Berkeley, CA.

A. Merc Rustad

A. Merc Rustad is a queer non-binary writer who lives in the Minnesota. Their stories have appeared in *Lightspeed, Fireside, Apex, Uncanny, Shimmer, Cicada,* and other fine venues. This year Merc is a Nebula Finalist! You can find Merc on Twitter @ Merc_Rustad, Patreon (https://www.patreon.com/mercrustad) or their website: http://amercrustad.com. Their debut short story collection, *SO YOU WANT TO BE A ROBOT,* is out from Lethe Press in May 2017.

Lucy A. Snyder

Lucy A. Snyder is a five-time Bram Stoker Award-winning writer who is the author of about 100 published short stories and ten books, including the erotica collection *Orchid Carousals.* Her writing has appeared in publications such as *Asimov's Science Fiction, Apex Magazine, Nightmare Magazine, Pseudopod, Strange Horizons,* and *Best Horror of the Year.* She lives in Ohio and is faculty in Seton Hill University's MFA program in Writing Popular Fiction. You can learn more about her at www.lucysnyder.com and you can follow her on Twitter at @LucyASnyder.

Lucien Soulban

Lucien Soulban got his start selling sex. He can tell you all about how he got started writing in the stone age of games with table-top RPGs and properties like *Vampire: The Masquerade* and *Dungeons & Dragons,* but his real first job was selling pornography to the other boys at his high school in the dark ages before the Internet and its bounty of free pornography. That's right, Lucien began his career as a smut peddler, bravely acting 18 when he was still only 13, and buying skin mags from the local convenience store clerk who either bought his "older than I look" act, or just didn't care that he was selling pornography to a minor. And when Lucien's customers demanded more specialized magazines, Lucien provided them with hardcore pictures at marked up prices until the day he graduated High School. Since making the jump to fiction, where he wrote novels for *Warhammer 40K* and *Dragonlance,* as well as various horror anthologies including *Blood Lite 1, 2, & 3, Streets of Shadow,* and *Dark Faith,* Lucien has been searching for a way to return to his roots... peddling little bits of filthy joy to an appreciative audience.

Molly Tanzer

Molly Tanzer is the author of forthcoming novel *Creatures of Will and Temper* (November 2017) as well as V*ermilion, The Pleasure Merchant,* and the British Fantasy and Wonderland Book Award-nominated collection *A Pretty Mouth.* Her short fiction has appeared in *Lightspeed Magazine, Nightmare Magazine, and Transcendent: The Year's Best Transgender and Genderqueer Speculative Fiction,* as well as many other locations. Her editorial projects include *Congress Magazine,* which publishes thoughtful erotica; she is also the co-editor of *Swords v Cthulhu* with Jesse Bullington, as well as the forthcoming *Mixed Up!* with Nick Mamatas (October 2017). She lives in Longmont, CO.

Tim Waggoner

Tim Waggoner has published over thirty novels and three short story collections, and his work has been nominated for the Shirley Jackson Award, the Bram Stoker Award, and the Scribe Award. He teaches creative writing at Sinclair College in Dayton, Ohio. You can find him on the web at www.timwaggoner.com

D.F. Warrick

D.F. Warrick is an American expatriate living in Leipzig, Germany. Their stories have appeared in *Tor.com, Apex Magazine, Daily Science Fiction,* and a bunch of other venues, and they contributed work to the recent PS4 hit *Horizon: Zero Dawn.* They enjoy sphinx cats, the *Alien* franchise, and hanging out in art squats with dirty punk rock kids almost half their age.

Jaye Wells

USA Today Bestseller Jaye Wells is a former magazine editor whose award-winning speculative fiction novels have hit several bestseller lists. She holds an MFA in Writing Popular Fiction from Seton Hill University, and is a sought-after speaker on the craft of writing. When she's not writing or teaching, she loves to travel to exotic locales, experiment in her kitchen like a mad scientist, and try things that scare her so she can write about them in her books. She lives in Texas. To learn more about her books, check out www.jayewells.com

THE EDITORS OF NASTY

Chris Phillips

Chris Phillips is the Managing Editor of *Flash Fiction Online.*

His work has appeared in *Orson Scott Card's Intergalactic Medicine Show (issues 48 & 52), Apex Magazine, Penumbra eMag, Sci Phi Journal,* and elsewhere. Chris holds an English degree from The Ohio State Univesity and an MFA from Seton Hill University.

Anna Yeatts

Anna Yeatts is the Publisher of *Flash Fiction Online,* one of the largest & oldest venues for short-short fiction.

Her short fiction has appeared in *Orson Scott Card's Intergalactic Medicine Show, Daily Science Fiction, Penumbra, Mslexia, & Cicada* among other publications. Follow her at annayeatts.com or on Twitter @AnnaYeatts.

NASTY Publications

NASTY Publications is looking for stories, novels, and novellas representing the spectrum of relationships between consenting adults.

Enthusiastic consent is a must.

We hope to fairly and without bias present the beauty of sensual relationships encompassing all sexual orientations, gender identities, gender expressions, races/ethnicities, religions, abilities, nationalities, and/or something not listed in this statement, as well as publish works by writers whose backgrounds are not well represented in the field of erotica and erotic romance.

Query letters plus the first ten pages of your novella should be emailed to novellasubs@thenastymag.com with the subject line: NASTY Novella - "Title"/Author Name. All novella samples should be formatted in standard manuscript format (12 point/Times New Roman, Arial, or Courier/double spaced/1" margins) sent as a .doc/.docx file.

For more specific information including payment, rights, and other more specialized submission calls visit NASTY Publications at thenastymag.com/submission-calls.

Made in the USA
Las Vegas, NV
26 September 2021